I let out a sound that was halfway between a gasp and a muted scream.

Think, Cybil.

I forced myself to walk to the body. Bending down, I moved my fingers up and down his throat but couldn't find a pulse. It was only then that I looked at the face and flinched. I knew that face, that person. I'd been assigned to follow him but I hadn't followed him closely enough and now he was dead.

I sank to my knees and stared helplessly, hopelessly.

Then I heard a stealthy sound, like someone moving carefully, slowly, to avoid making a noise. My body froze, wondering if a knife was inches from being plunged into my back. No! I wasn't going to wait to become another victim. With a cry I hoped sounded ferocious, I jumped up and turned, ready to lunge at whoever was behind me, but all I saw was the emergency door to the outside closing fast.

★

ALIBI FOR A COLD WINTER'S NIGHT

ILSA MAYR

TORONTO • NEW YORK • LONDON
AMSTERDAM • PARIS • SYDNEY • HAMBURG
STOCKHOLM • ATHENS • TOKYO • MILAN
MADRID • WARSAW • BUDAPEST • AUCKLAND

ALIBI FOR A COLD WINTER'S NIGHT

A Worldwide Mystery/November 2011

First published by Avalon Books

ISBN-13: 978-0-373-26777-4

Copyright © 2008 by Ilsa Dallmayr

To my husband for his love and support.

ONE

THE ONLY SOUND I HEARD in the stillness peculiar to softly falling snow on an early winter morning was the crunching of my boots. I loved that sound and the stillness which was as peaceful and reverential as that of a gothic cathedral. Though it was still too dark to see clearly, I knew the bare branches of the trees would look as if sprinkled with powdered sugar. Westport, Indiana, would enjoy a winter wonderland kind of a day.

I parked my car in the area assigned to employees and volunteers of Mercy Shelter, the one located the farthest from the building. On most Saturdays, my day to volunteer, the lot was empty this time of the morning except for the shelter's elderly pickup, a beat-up vehicle held together by mismatched parts and fervent prayers—or curses, depending on who was driving it. Today was no exception. The pickup sat in its customary spot.

As I got closer to the truck, I heard its engine running. That didn't make sense. Who'd be warming it up this early? I squinted through the white curtain of the falling snow. Why was the parking lot so dark? We had improved the lighting just before Thanksgiving by adding two tall security street lamps. I looked up and stopped walking. How could a new lamp be burned out already? After what the shelter paid for it? Wait till I get IJ Electric on the phone. I was not only a volunteer, but a newly appointed member of the shelter's board of directors and thus involved with its always-lean budget and troubled finances.

Resolutely, I rushed toward the truck. When I was a few feet away, the motor sputtered and died. In the sudden silence my steps faltered. Something was behind the wheel. Something big. I couldn't see clearly because of the snow which clung to the window.

"Is someone in the truck?" I called out.

Silence.

I took a step forward and yelled, "Hello? Anyone in there?"

No answer.

I stepped closer. I wiped away the powdery snow from the window and jumped back with a cry of alarm. What had merely been a large dark suggestion of something behind the wheel was the form of a man.

I knocked on the window even though in my gut I suspected the man was beyond responding. During my time as an apprentice private investigator in my uncle's security agency I had come across several dead bodies, and though each one had died in a different manner they all shared something indefinable. An absence. An emptiness.

Grasping the door handle, I yanked, but the door was locked. I ran to the passenger side but that door wouldn't open. I looked around for something heavy I could use to break the window, but everything was frozen and covered with snow. There was only one thing to do—get the spare key from the office. I ran to the back door, fumbling with my key ring, and finally managed to unlock the door and switch on the light in the hall. I retrieved the spare key from the office.

Just then Darnell, the night watchman, who had obviously been taking a nap in the study, stumbled into the hall. "What's going on, Mrs. Quindt?" he asked.

"Someone's locked inside the truck," I said, running past him.

"In our truck? On a freezing cold night like tonight? The heater ain't even working good. And how did he get the key to the truck?"

I couldn't take the time to reply. He grabbed his parka and followed me outside as fast as his gimpy leg allowed. When I managed to unlock the door after a couple of tries, he looked over my shoulder.

"Chico, is that you? What the heck you doing out here, man?" Darnell asked. "And how did you get this old heap started?"

I took off my glove, and placing my fingers against Chico's throat I searched for a sign of life. There was none.

"Is he dead?" Darnell whispered.

"I think so. I can't find a pulse." I took the cell phone from my shoulder bag and dialed 911. "Don't touch anything," I told Darnell. "Just in case."

"Just in case of what?"

A good question. Surely the man had died from exposure or poor nutrition or lack of medical care. Why had I even wondered if this was anything but an unfortunate but natural death? Or at worse, an accidental death? I shut the truck's door carefully.

BECAUSE OF ITS DOWNTOWN location, Mercy Shelter was only a few blocks from the police station as well as from Westport Central Hospital. The black-and-white unit and the ambulance arrived one right after the other. Even though we had been outside for only a short time, both Darnell and I were chilled to the bone. We stamped our feet and beat our arms.

After I briefly explained how I had found Chico, the officer in charge took pity on us and told us to wait inside the shelter.

In the kitchen I put on a small pot of coffee before I got the two big percolators going. The reason I'd come to the shelter so early was to help cook breakfast for the thirty people who'd found a bed for the night in the dormitory and the crowd of homeless who'd stand in line at seven for a hot meal.

While I waited for the coffeemaker to do its thing, I looked at the fingers clutching the edge of the counter in a death grip. It took a moment for me to realize that they were mine. As I made myself let go of the counter, I realized I didn't need the stimulation of coffee but the soothing effects of herbal tea.

For my last birthday, Luke, my estranged husband, had given me a lovely enameled box the size of a small paperback book filled with herbal tea bags. I took one out and dropped it into a tall mug. Then I put fresh water into the tea kettle and put it on to boil.

I had taken only a few sips of tea when the officers entered the kitchen. I offered them coffee which they gratefully accepted. Then they asked me to tell them again how I had found Chico. I noticed that they interviewed Darnell separately. To compare our stories? They told me that I needed to come downtown to make a statement.

"Can I come later? Around nine? We're going to have a bunch of hungry people here in about an hour who'll be very disappointed if there's no warm food."

Sergeant Griffin told me nine o'clock would be fine.

I took two cartons of eggs from the fridge. When I cracked the first one, part of the shell fell into the big bowl because my hands weren't steady. I told myself to relax. I took a couple of deep breaths but no matter how hard I tried I could not erase the image of the dead man from my mind. Suddenly my knees felt weak. I had to pull out one of the tall counter stools to sit down. This would never do. *How could I fix French toast for seventy-plus people when my hands were trembling?*

"Cybil? Where are you?" said the welcome voice of the shelter's director, Abigail Sorensen.

"I'm over here, Abby."

"Are you okay?" she asked.

"I thought I was, but now I'm not so sure. My hands are shaking."

"Well, why wouldn't they? Finding a dead man in our truck? Mercy me. How awful for you." She pulled out a stool and sat down beside me. "The police phoned me."

"I should have called. I'm sorry." Then I proceeded to tell Abby what had happened.

"I know Chico," she said. "He's been coming to the shelter since the middle of October. It's been too cold to sleep outside. Poor man. I suppose he kept the motor running to stay warm. How did he get the key?"

"The key?" I walked to the drawer where we kept the truck's keys. I took both of them out and held them up for Abby to see. "This is the one I took to unlock the truck and this one with the tag is the spare key."

"Then how did he start the truck?"

"He must have hot-wired it. I don't know how to do it, but Chico apparently did."

"Did he have a heart attack?"

"I don't know." I put both keys back into the drawer.

"You don't suppose the heater stopped working completely and he froze to death?" Abby shuddered visibly.

"I've never seen a person who died from exposure, but when I touched his neck he didn't seem that cold." I thought for a moment. "Could the fumes have gotten to him?"

"You mean carbon monoxide poisoning? Oh, Lord." Abby clasped her hands so tightly her knuckles turned white. "I should have bought a better truck instead of getting the roof fixed."

"If you hadn't fixed the leaky roof, the ceiling in here would have fallen down before Thanksgiving," I pointed out.

She grabbed a handful of her short salt-and-pepper hair and pulled. It was a gesture of stress and frustration that always made me wince.

"Why don't we ever have enough money to run this shelter properly?" she wailed.

"Because we operate with soft money and donations. We never know exactly how much we'll have for any given month and that makes it hard to plan. But you're doing a great job with what we have," I said and meant it. "You can make a dollar bill go further than anybody I know."

"Thank you, Cybil," she murmured, pleased and embarrassed at the same time.

Abby used to be a nun. She still lived like one, except that she now wore jeans and flannel shirts instead of a dark blue skirt, white blouse, and a wimple.

I poured her a cup of coffee, noticing that my hands had stopped trembling. Talking to Abby made me feel better. She had that effect on most people. I resumed breaking eggs into the bowl.

"What can I do to help?" she asked.

"You could get the bread slices ready. The griddle should be hot enough in a minute or two."

Abby took the packages of day-old bread I'd bought cheaply at the bakery and piled them on a platter. Stale bread made better French toast, as fresh bread had a tendency to fall apart in the egg mixture.

From my purse I took the bottle of vanilla extract I'd brought from home and added a couple of generous splashes to the eggs.

"We can't even afford to buy a bottle of vanilla," Abby said bitterly.

She was really down. Ordinarily such a small thing wouldn't have bothered her.

"Our Christmas bazaar and cookie walk starts next week. That'll replenish our bank account," I said, my voice consoling. "I bet we take in enough so we can splurge and buy a whole gallon of vanilla. And a case of syrup. Then we can serve pancakes again."

She nodded. "You're right. We've already received

a bunch of craft items. Let's hope our cookie donations will be generous."

"You can count on me and on my grandmother.
We both like to bake. My mom will probably write
a check. She's not into baking." That was an understatement. My mother entered her state-of-the-art
kitchen only if she absolutely could not avoid it. Or
to give her cook instructions. It's not that she can't
cook. Maxi, my grandmother, taught her when Mom
was a teenager, just as she had taught me. I used to
think that Mom hated to cook, but in recent years
I've come to suspect that she stays out of the kitchen
primarily to avoid food and keep her reed-thin figure. Looking good is very important to her. Maybe
that's the curse suffered by women who are born
breathtakingly beautiful and to whom it is of the ut-
most importance that they look stunning every minute of every day.

"Your mom's check will be welcome. We'll use it
to buy staple goods for the kitchen. With the winter
months facing us, we'll need every ounce of food
we can stockpile. The way heating costs have gone
up, a lot of people will have less money for groceries."

Abby was right, unfortunately. During the next
three months we'd be feeding more people than ever
before. But I had no time to pursue that line of worry.
The griddle was hot, and I could hear hungry people
lining up outside.

I PUSHED THE FOUR QUARTERS I'd found in my purse into the parking meter, hoping my stay at the police station would be a short one. When the first person I ran into was Lieutenant Sam Keller, my cousin, I knew this wasn't going to be a quick trip.

"Cybil, what are you doing here?" he asked with a frown. "Something wrong? With Maxi?"

"No. Oma's fine. I came to sign a statement."

"Oh, no. Not you. You're the one who found the dead man at the shelter? I should have known. Only you'd find a corpse in a truck on a cold morning."

Sam's voice had taken on that long-suffering tone I knew so well. "You make it sound as if I'm always doing macabre things." He didn't reply verbally but the look he gave me spoke volumes.

"Come on," he said not too graciously, at the same time rubbing his eyes which were red and tired.

"Is the baby still keeping you up nights, teething?"

"No. I pulled a double shift yesterday. I'm getting too old for that."

I stopped myself just in time from offering to lend him money to keep him from working two shifts. Sam was a proud man and my offer would have insulted him. I'd talk to Maxi. If anyone could find out if he had money problems without hurting his feelings, it was my grandmother. Not that either of us had tons of money but Maxi had always lived frugally and I no longer had anyone to spend money on. Not since I lost my sweet little boy.

Memories sliced through me. I concentrated on breathing deeply to keep the pain endurable. Fortunately we'd reached Sam's office where he started to fire questions at me and wrote down my answers.

"When you unlocked the truck, what did you see?"

"A man sitting behind the wheel who didn't respond. I felt for a pulse and then called for help."

"Anything else?"

"I thought he must have hot-wired the truck, but I didn't know that for sure until I found both keys in the drawer where we kept them."

"What did you touch?"

"I was wearing gloves. It was freezing cold, remember? I only took one glove off when I searched for his pulse." I looked at Sam carefully. Something wasn't right with these questions. "What's wrong? Isn't this just an accidental death?" His expression confirmed my suspicion. "What makes you think it wasn't an accident?"

"I don't know. Something's a little off." Sam took a slip of paper and handed it to me.

I read it out loud: "'Set thine house in order.' Sounds Biblical. What about it?"

"We found it in Chico's coat pocket. Did he get it at the shelter?"

"I'm sure he didn't. We don't preach at the shel-

ter." I read the quote again. "I guess it could be considered a threat. Is that what you're getting at?"

Sam shrugged. "Did Chico have enemies?"

"I have no idea. I didn't really know him. Why
don't you ask the other men at the shelter? Abby said
Chico had been a regular since October."

"Oh, we've asked. Most of the men disappear into
the woodwork when we appear and the few we've
managed to talk to claim to know nothing."

"You can't blame them. For most of them their
only contact with the cops has been confrontational.
You're always telling them to move on."

"The mayor thinks they're an embarrassment to
the city."

"An embarrassment?" I sputtered. The mayor
wasn't one of my favorite people. His programs to
improve Westport moved with the speed of a sleepy
two-toed sloth, and he hadn't kept a single one of his
campaign promises. Not that this was unusual for a
politician but I had expected better from him.

"If his honor doesn't like to see them hanging out
on the street, then why doesn't he provide places for
them to live?" I snapped. "There are several empty
buildings in the neighborhood that could be converted into SROs. The city could probably buy them
for a dollar and back taxes."

"Don't yell at me. I'm all for a single-room occupancy program."

I sighed. "I'm sorry but the homeless are a real

touchy subject with me." I glanced at my watch. "I'm meeting Maxi for a late breakfast. Is there anything else?"

"No, but keep your eyes and ears open at the shelter. If you hear anything, let me know."

I said I would.

MAXI WAS ALREADY SEATED in a booth when I got to the Clover Bar and Grill, the coffee shop of the restored, historic Nightingale Hotel. I kissed her cheek and sat down across from her.

"What's wrong, Schatzi?" she asked.

I opened my mouth and shut it. "I was going to ask what made you think something was wrong, but you'd only smile mysteriously and give me one of those elegant little European shrugs. Somehow you always know."

Maxi smiled. "When I was a girl in Vienna, we, the teenaged girls, had a whole repertoire of nonverbal ways we used to communicate with, or confuse, the young men around us."

"I bet you were a master in this nonverbal exchange."

"I think I had my moments," Maxi said with a grin.

The waitress came to take our order. We came here so often that we didn't have to look at the menu. We both ordered omelets. Maxi wanted potatoes with hers and I grits. This cafe was the only place in West-port, Indiana, where I could get this southern treat.

"So, tell me. It's not nice to keep an old lady wait-ing."

Though Maxi was in her seventies and her body was frail-looking, her mind was sharp and her spirit indomitable. I told her about Chico.

"The poor man. And poor you for being the one to find him. What a way to start the day."

"I still can't believe that someone would sit in a car with the engine running and not open the win-dow a crack."

"It was bitterly cold last night. He might have been thoroughly chilled when he sat down in the truck and opening a window would have been the farthest thing from his mind."

"And he wasn't dressed all that warmly either," I added. "What do you make of the quotation? It's from the Bible, isn't it?"

"Yes. Kings. Second Book," said Maxi, who knew her Bible well.

"Was it meant to be a threat?"

"The original quotation was certainly a warning. 'Set thine house in order for you shall die.'"

"Why would someone threaten Chico? He had al-most nothing, and from what Darnell indicated, he got along with the other men at the shelter."

Maxi pondered this a moment. "This may not have been a direct or specific threat but just a general warning. You know, the kind that some hellfire and brimstone preachers hurl at their congregations from the pulpit on Sunday mornings."

"What if it wasn't? We can't let someone intimidate our people at the shelter," I exclaimed.

"No, we can't. What do you know about Chico?"

"Very little."

"Before we can make a reasonable guess about the motive, we have to find out all about Chico. He was around the shelter long enough to have become friendly with someone."

"I wonder where he was before. What kind of life he'd led. Abby forbids prying questions."

"As she should. Questions might keep some of the men from coming back," Maxi pointed out.

We ate for a while. Then I asked, "How old do you think Chico was?"

"In his early sixties but he could have been younger. It's difficult to judge because life on the street is hard. And the lack of proper medical and dental care doesn't help."

"If some religious nut has singled out the shelter—"

"That's why we have to work fast," Maxi said.

"We?"

"Yes, we. You'll need help. Tomorrow's my day to cook breakfast. I'll hang around and see what I can find out. I'm a harmless old lady. People usually talk to me." Maxi's bright blue eyes sparkled.

"You, harmless?" I snorted. It was a good thing my mother wasn't there to hear that most unladylike sound. "You want me to come and help you?"

"Thank you for offering but I can manage. Don't you have to bake cookies?"

I'd forgotten about the cookies. "Yes. I suppose you've already baked yours?"

"Well, the *Lebkuchen* need to age so the honey softens and the spices ripen. And the others freeze well. At my age you have to do things on the days when you feel well."

I looked at her, alarmed, knowing that one day I'd lose her. I always prayed that this dreadful day was in the distant future. I didn't think I could survive losing another person I loved any time soon.

"How is Luke? Have you seen him recently?" she asked casually.

Maxi adored my husband, and I was sure she would like nothing better than to see us reconciled. "He's fine. Puts in too many hours at the hospital, but that's par for the course."

"He's a talented, dedicated, and conscientious doctor," she said, her voice approving.

He certainly was that. Also bossy and stubborn and controlling—qualities I found harder to like as I got older. Not that almost thirty was really old. But old enough to know that I wanted to make my own decisions and choose the career I wanted. Luke didn't think much of me being an apprentice PI at the Keller Security Agency owned by my uncle.

As we had finished our food and as I didn't want to talk about Luke, I said, "I have to go to the food bank to get our allotment for the shelter, and I have to go to the grocery store before I can bake cookies. I know I need butter and eggs."

AFTER I COLLECTED THE groceries from the city's central food bank, I took them to the shelter. Several of the regular clients were standing against the back wall, smoking and talking. The shelter was closed to them during the day, forcing them to find refuge elsewhere. I asked for help in unloading the cartons.

The man I'd heard called Pete was the first to volunteer. He was a quiet man, polite, soft-spoken with a spark of intelligence and humor in his eyes. I wondered what sort of work he'd done before ending up on the street. I couldn't ask, of course. Even if it hadn't been against shelter policy, I wouldn't have intruded on his privacy.

While we were stacking cartons, I asked, "Did you know Chico?"

"Yes. We spoke sometimes."

"Do you know if he had any family we should notify of his passing?"

"You might ask Earl, who probably knew Chico best." Pete shook his head. "But even if he had someone, he wouldn't have wanted them to know where he'd ended up. Once you're on the street the past is dead. There's only the here and now. Such as it is."

I know I stared at Pete for a long moment. I'd never heard this sentiment before, but then my main interest in the shelter's clients had been to supply them with nourishing meals. Odd, Pete hadn't sounded bitter, just resigned.

"I'm still wondering how Chico ended up in the truck," I said. "He was one of the regulars who came early to get a bed."

Pete paused, holding a carton of canned goods. "Yes, it's even stranger that he knew how to hot-wire a car when he couldn't even drive one."

TWO

"MAY I PLEASE SPEAK with Lieutenant Keller? This is Cybil Quindt. Yes, I'll hold."

Sam picked up the phone a minute later. "Hey, cuz. What's up?"

"What are you eating?" I asked, knowing he was on a strict diet to lose fifteen pounds and hopefully lower his cholesterol.

"Just one small egg roll."

"From the place on the corner?" I asked, my voice horrified.

"Yeah. And it's filled with vegetables," he added virtuously.

"And it's deep fried which cancels the value of the veggies."

"What are you? My food censor?"

"You need one. But that's not why I called. I just found out that Chico didn't know how to drive a car. What are the chances of a man who didn't know how to drive being able to hot-wire a car?"

There was a lengthy silence. I could picture Sam wiping his greasy fingers on a small paper napkin, his forehead wrinkled in thought.

"It's not likely," he finally said. "But not impossible. He could have picked up the skill of hot-wiring on the street."

"Would you run his name through the License Bureau database, please, just to be sure."

"I guess I can do that. Is there anything specific that makes you think this wasn't an accidental death? Something you forgot to mention?" he asked, his tone suspicious.

"No. Just a sense of unease."

"That's probably because you found the body."

He could be right. "Let me know what you find out about Chico's license." I hung up and went into the dining room to inspect how good a job the men had done on wiping the tables and sweeping the floor. We maintained a roster of men who did these tasks in exchange for a guaranteed bed at night.

A woman I'd seen around the shelter recently was in the dining room, taking the chairs off the tables where the men had placed them to make sweeping easier.

"Your turn to work?" I asked.

She nodded.

"My name is Cybil Quindt. And yours is?"

She didn't answer right away and from the expression on her face I thought she might not.

"Duchess. I'm known as Duchess."

"Nice to meet you," I said and smiled at her encouragingly. Her voice was low and gritty as if she rarely used it or had smoked a pack of cigarettes a day for most of her life. As we continued to work, I studied her surreptitiously. We didn't get many women at the shelter and always reserved the attic bedroom for them.

Duchess wore a man's overcoat, which obviously was too big for her. She'd rolled up the sleeves so that the frayed lining showed and had tied a piece of rope around her middle. The dark gray garment bloused above the makeshift belt. I saw her repeatedly whisper down into the unbuttoned collar. At first I thought she was one of the homeless who spoke to make-believe friends but when I discovered that something moved under the coat I changed my mind.

For a terrifying moment I wondered if she had a baby strapped to her chest. I studied her face. No, even if life on the street had aged her prematurely she was well beyond her childbearing years. My second guess was that she had a pet. My heart went out to her. It had to be incredibly hard to survive on the street herself but to take care of a pet?

"How's your pet, Duchess?"

She gasped and placed her hands protectively over her chest.

"It's okay. I won't tell anyone. May I see her? Him?"

"Her. Buddy."

Duchess reached inside her coat and pulled out the most bedraggled-looking kitten I had ever seen. On second glance I saw that the orange tabby had only one eye. I must have stared at the poor little thing.

"She was hurt bad when I found her. The vet over on Main Street said she couldn't do nothin' about Buddy's eye except clean it up. She gave me some medicine so it wouldn't get infected. She was real nice to Buddy."

Duchess looked at her pet with so much love that tears pooled in my eyes. I cleared my throat. "Would Buddy like something to eat?"

The woman nodded solemnly. "Buddy could eat. She's always hungry."

"Let's see what we can find in the kitchen." There wasn't much in the fridge but Buddy wasn't a fussy eater. She practically inhaled the hot dog I'd cut up into tiny pieces and eagerly lapped the milk I'd poured into a cereal bowl. I made a mental note to buy a bag of kitten chow and keep it in the office.

"Tomorrow my grandmother, Maxi, will do the cooking. You know her?"

"The small, nice lady with all that white hair?"

Maxi's hair was white and thick, she was small in stature, and she certainly was nice and a lady in the best sense of the word. "That's her. I'll tell her about Buddy, so after breakfast come back here and she'll have food for your kitty."

"God bless you," Duchess said and wiped her hand over her eyes.

"Thank you," I murmured. I'd take all the blessings I could get. Impulsively I took out a business card. "If Buddy ever needs help please give me a call." I wrote my home phone number on the back and handed her the card.

She nodded her thanks. She adjusted the bag she carried slung over her shoulder. It reminded me of an old-fashioned carpetbag. Undoubtedly it held her few belongings.

"I better go or the warmest spots will be taken. Buddy don't like the cold."

I assumed Duchess referred to the empty building next to the church two blocks away where the homeless spent part of their day. The people from the church could afford to turn the heat on for only half a day, but it was dry and offered protection from the wind and the snow.

She put the kitten back inside her coat and shuffled off. She always moved as if each step hurt. I looked at her feet which were stuck in ill-fitting men's shoes that were held together with masking tape. The sight of that tape broke the restraints that had held my anger in check for a long time. I picked up a big wooden spoon and smashed it against the kitchen counter until it splintered, all the while muttering unkind things with each whack.

"Feel better?"

I knew that voice. During our courting days it had caused me to catch my breath. Even now its pleasant timbre fell comfortingly on my ears.

"What did that spoon do to you that it deserves being thwacked and sworn at in German?" Luke asked, sounding amused as well as concerned. "What's wrong?"

I shrugged. "Everything. We never have enough money for what we need. Food. Beds. Warm clothing. Medical care. We live in one of the richest countries in the world, so why can't we take care of people who need it? And Duchess's shoes are held together by tape and Buddy has only one eye—"

"Who's Buddy?"

"Her kitten. Duchess has nothing except that kitten and both may die in this cold and I can't...I can't..." I lost it then. Collapsing on the kitchen stool, I threw my arms on the counter and buried my face against them and wept. This was no soft, ladylike weeping but loud, keening sounds that tore from my throat.

"Cybil."

Luke pulled me into his arms and held me. He didn't say it was dumb to cry. He didn't offer any platitudes, and he was astute enough not to mention PMS. He stroked my hair and let me weep until I had no more tears.

I freed myself from his arms. I tore off a section from the roll of paper towels and dried my eyes. "I'm sorry. I don't know what made me fall apart like that."

"Stress comes to mind. And compassion. You're

basically a softy, taking on the misery of the whole world. It's one of the things I've always loved about you."

I stopped myself from asking if there still was something else he loved about me. Such a question might suggest I was fishing for a compliment or worse, sending the wrong message. I was not ready for overtures toward a reconciliation. Sometimes I wondered if I ever would be. We couldn't go back to the way things were before our little boy died. That had changed everything irrevocably, but Luke didn't see that.

At the sink I splashed cold water on my face. Luke handed me a paper towel. He yawned and shook his head as if to shake off extreme tiredness.

"You didn't just now get off duty, did you?"

"I did. The emergency room was full all night. Several car accidents. A bad one on the toll road. Why people don't slow down when it's snowing I'll never understand."

"It was the first big snow of the season. People forget that they need to drive slower." I looked at him again. "Is there a special reason why you stopped by?"

"Yeah. I was wondering if you're going to Maxi's farm for her Saint Nicholas Day lunch?"

"Yes. Are you?"

"Of course. Would I miss one of your grandmother's meals?" he asked and grinned.

At that moment he looked so much like the med student he was the first time I saw him that something inside me seemed to shift.

"You want to drive to the farm with me?" he asked.

"Uncle Barney is going too. We could all go together." I knew I was sort of weaseling out, but if we all went together nobody would get the message that Luke and I were a couple again. I risked a quick glance at him. If he was disappointed he didn't show it.

"Good idea. Ask Barney if he minds my going along."

"He won't mind, but I'll ask." Uncle Barney liked Luke a lot. But then there wasn't a single member of my extended family who didn't.

"I'll walk you to your car," Luke offered.

WHEN I PARKED IN FRONT of my house, I took a moment to look at it fondly. With the sprinkling of new snow it looked a little bit like an enchanted miniature castle. The real estate people had listed it as a fixer upper, Luke referred to it as a Victorian wreck, and Maxi called it a house with character and a past. I liked her description best.

A month ago I had replaced all the windows which had effectively wiped out my savings, but I'd had no choice. I knew I wasn't tough enough to survive a northern Indiana winter in a house with an overabundance of tall windows, all of which seemed determined to let in as much cold air as possible. All other house improvements on my list had to wait until I'd replenished my savings.

Each time Luke saw the house his expression grew grim, but he was smart enough not to say anything. At least most of the time. Not my mother, though. Ever since I bought the house a short time before my undercover work in the bank, she's been offering to pay for repairs and remodeling. Last time I saw her, I had to threaten to stop speaking to her if she didn't cease and desist. Even Uncle Barney, who rarely commented on my personal life, offered a loan against my future salary. Only Maxi hadn't criticized or offered money, though I had no doubt that she'd mortgage her farm in a heartbeat if I needed financial help.

I carried the groceries to the kitchen which faced the backyard. This was my favorite room in the house and the one I'd done the most work on. I had painted the glass-fronted cabinets a pleasing shade of green and the walls a warm ochre. Under the dingy carpet that someone in the seventies had tacked onto the floor, I discovered a lovely layer of wood. After a thorough cleaning and waxing, the rich patina of the wood gleamed warmly. I protected the high-traffic area with rag rugs Maxi had woven for me.

I brewed a pot of Darjeeling tea and enjoyed drinking it at my kitchen table.

ON SUNDAY MORNING my plans for sleeping in were rudely shattered by the ringing of the phone. Groggily I sat up and reached for the receiver. An official voice asked me to come to the morgue to identify an old woman's body.

My heart stopped beating for a moment. "No! It can't be my grandmother. It can't. What makes you think it is her?"

"We're not sure who the woman is but we found your business card in her coat pocket. There was no other ID. That's why we phoned you."

The room seemed to be spinning. Why would Maxi have my business card in her pocket? She knew the agency's number as well as my home and cell phone numbers by heart.

"We believe this woman is…was one of the homeless who spent time around Mercy Shelter."

Relief washed over me with such a force that I fell back against my pillow. The relief was almost immediately followed by a wave of guilt. "Duchess. It's Duchess."

"How soon can you get here? And do you know where the morgue is?"

"Isn't it in the old building behind Westport Central Hospital?"

"Yes. Come to the back door and ring the bell."

"I'll be there in fifteen minutes."

Because I shivered and my teeth chattered—probably more due to the receding adrenaline than the cold—I threw on several layers of clothes. I even managed to brush my teeth and gather my hair into a ponytail, all the while wondering what had happened. Since we kept the attic room at the shelter for women, there was always a bed for all who came. Why hadn't Duchess come in out of the cold?

Maybe she had. Maybe she'd suffered a fatal stroke or heart attack. Most likely it was the cold, though. According to the television weatherman, the cold wave we'd been hit with since right after Thanksgiving was the most severe in recent history.

Since parking around the hospital was problematic, I decided to jog to the morgue and back. *This could qualify as my formal exercise for the day,* I told myself smugly. Luke had pointed out the location of the morgue when he'd given me the tour of the hospital at the time he was put in charge of the emergency room services.

I jogged at a good clip until I got close to the place. Then my steps slowed until they grew uncertain. Pausing in front of the door, I suddenly wanted to turn and run back home. Calling myself a coward, I pressed the doorbell as instructed. The slow, dragging footsteps I heard conjured up a vision of a Boris Karloff-like creature getting ready to fling open the door and pounce on me. I think I might have whimpered. I dislike horror films because I fall for every shlocky special effect and end up watching most of the film with my hands pressed over my eyes.

When the door finally opened—and it didn't even creak—I came face to face with a short, elderly man, whose silvery fringe of hair stood up around his head like the bristles of a worn-out brush. His right foot was encased in a bootlike cast, which explained the dragging sound. He squinted at me through bottle-thick glasses.

"Come in," he said. "Sorry you had to wait, but on Sundays there's only a skeleton crew on duty at the morgue." He cackled. "Get it?"

I nodded. "Skeleton crew. Morgue." I smiled weakly, wondering just how much macabre morgue humor I'd have to listen to.

"I'm Mr. Knell."

I looked at him, startled. Was he joking? Knell? As in death knell? But he seemed to be serious. More than ever I wanted to turn around and run home.

"Follow me," he said, his voice commanding.

I did, reluctantly, all the time hoping I'd be able to view the body on a television screen. As soon as we entered a room with metal drawers built into the wall, I knew I'd have to identify the body up close and personal.

Mercifully, most of the experience was a blur, but I do remember thinking how small Duchess looked lying on the metal surface.

In the office I had to answer more questions and sign more forms. Finally, when I could leave the building, I ran outside and gulped in air as if I'd been in danger of suffocating. I didn't even notice how cold that air was until it made my eyes water and my lungs ache.

I wish I could claim that I remembered the kitten immediately but I didn't. Not until I was halfway home. I ran back to the morgue and rang the bell frantically.

"Now what?" Mr. Knell asked crankily.

"Duchess had a kitten. A small, one-eyed orange tabby. Was it brought here with her?"

Her drew himself up to his full height but still had to look up at me. "Only dead bodies are allowed in here. And only homo sapiens. Call the animal shelter over on Oak Street."

"Thanks." Why hadn't I thought of that? Or remembered the kitten earlier?

From my house I phoned the animal shelter. They had no orange kittens. Hadn't had any since early September. Discouraged, I put the phone down. Now what? Maybe Duchess had left Buddy at Mercy Shelter. Knowing that everyone would be too busy with breakfast to answer the phone, I drove there.

Maxi was dishing out food to the last of the breakfast clients.

"We ran out of toast, so I had to use some of the rolls we're serving for dinner tonight. I better go to the store to buy some more." She looked at me. "What's wrong?"

I told her about having to identify Duchess.

"I'm so sorry, Schatzi. That couldn't have been a pleasant experience."

"Now I'm worried about Buddy. The one-eyed orange kitten, remember? Have you seen her?"

"No, but let's ask the men. Maybe one of them saw her."

Maxi picked up and rang the small bell we used whenever we wanted the attention of our clients. They liked Maxi and listened to her respectfully but no one had seen Buddy. Pete suggested that since Duchess used to bring the kitten to the church house on Ohio Street, she might be hanging out around there.

I thanked him. Then, turning to Maxi, I asked for advice on how I could catch the kitten.

"As you know, I'm allergic to cats, so when your mother was little she could never bring any of our barn cats into the house. She used to play with them outside. Whenever she wanted to lure a particularly shy one out from her hiding spot, she'd take an open can of tuna. Sooner or later the aroma would prove too seductive."

I glanced at my grandmother to see if she was serious. "You want me to walk through the neighborhood with a can of tuna and call 'Buddy, here Buddy?'"

"Yes, if you're serious about finding her, but calling her name might not do the trick. She might not know her name yet, so you're better off calling 'Here, kitty, kitty.'"

Rather than drive all the way home, I walked to the nearby convenience store and bought a can of tuna. When I asked the high school kid behind the counter to open it for me he gave me a sneering look and said, "We don't do that. You have to buy a can opener."

"Aren't you one of the Milligan boys?" I asked in my best high school counselor's voice. With the typical Milligan overbite, freckles, and red hair, he had to be a member of that large boisterous family. Most of them had passed through my office with great frequency when I was a counselor.

"Yeah." His upper lip curled into a sneer but under my unwavering gaze he decided to open the can.

"Thank you," I said with my sweetest smile that deflated some of his teenage bravado.

Since my mother had chosen to marry a series of fussy, fastidious but wealthy men, I had never had a pet of my own. To say that I felt a little foolish walking down the street with a can of tuna, calling to a kitten, is putting it mildly. I had covered the two-block area several times without sight of the kitten when it occurred to me to concentrate on the church house.

It was built on concrete slabs, which created a crawl space. I lay facedown next to the gas meter where the snow had left an opening to the crawl space, placed the tuna in front of me, and softly called the kitten. Silence. I called again and waited. Nothing. What if I'd come too late? It had been awfully cold last night. I called again and again until I finally heard a rustling sound of something moving. Of course, it could be rats or some other small animals, but I couldn't give up until I knew for sure Buddy wasn't there.

The soft sounds came closer. Moments later I looked into a little bewhiskered face whose one golden eye considered me warily. I didn't move. I hardly breathed. Buddy sniffed, took a step closer, snatched a mouthful of tuna, retreated a step, and ate. She continued this way, eating rapidly. As her first hunger was stilled, Buddy slowed down and stopped retreating.

When she was finished I grabbed her by the scruff of her neck the way Maxi told me and picked her up. She hung from my hand totally relaxed as if her mother were carrying her in her mouth. I put Buddy inside my parka the way Duchess had and set out for the vet's office.

I used my cell phone to alert them that I was on my way.

The vet, a thirtysomething pretty redhead, addressed Buddy with a soothing voice and examined her with gentle hands.

"No fleas. No ear mites. That's good." She looked at Buddy's missing eye. "Healing nicely," she said pleased. She used her stethoscope, probed and poked, and finally pronounced Buddy to be in good shape, though a little too thin and a tad small for her age. Dr. Laura administered the first set of immunizations. We scheduled the next appointment, and I took the kitten home in a carrier I bought at the clinic.

Rather than let Buddy get lost in my large two-story house, I confined her to the butler's pantry and the laundry room. Besides, since they're located next to the kitchen, these rooms were the warmest in the house.

I would have to go shopping for a proper litter box but in the meantime I filled a low-sided carton with newspaper torn into strips. Buddy used the box, intuitively knowing what it was for. She finished with a lot of energetic digging in the paper.

I set out a bowl of water and one of dry kitten food. Not knowing what kittens likes to sleep on, I placed a throw pillow and a folded old chenille bedspread on either side of the heat register. Buddy could choose which she preferred. I left her washing herself. When I checked on her fifteen minutes later, she was curled into a tight ball, sound asleep on the bedspread. If I hadn't been afraid of waking her I would have stroked her silken fur.

MONDAY AND TUESDAY I spent at the agency writing reports on two cases we had finished. One involved a deadbeat dad and the other a credit check requested by a local business.

Every day at lunch I dashed home to check on Buddy. She seemed glad to see me. At least that's what I told myself. While I ate at my kitchen table, I put a little of my plain yogurt in a cup which I set down next to my chair. She ate it with obvious enjoyment.

When I got back to the agency on Wednesday, Lynn Nguyen, our receptionist and resident grouch, stopped me.

"The police here again. What you do now?" she hissed in her accented voice, her dark, almond-shaped eyes looking at me with undisguised disapproval.

Lynn didn't like any female whom Uncle Barney liked. Since he and I were related by blood I was no threat to her, but Lynn didn't see it that way. She was irrational where Uncle Barney was concerned. They met when he was stationed in Vietnam during the war. I always suspected that they were lovers then. I didn't know if their present relationship went beyond employer and employee but I knew they didn't live together.

"Where are the cops?" I asked, ignoring her disapproval.

"In your office. And you gone longer than thirty minutes for lunch." She looked pointedly at her wrist watch.

She would have loved to dock me for that infraction but since I didn't punch a time clock she couldn't. I hurried upstairs.

Sergeant Griffin stood by the window. He turned when I entered.

"We need you to come to the station."

Since he said this without his usual courteous inquiries about my health I knew this was serious.

THREE

AS THE SERGEANT AND I walked past Lynn's desk she jumped up and confronted us.

"Where you go? You under arrest?"

I knew Lynn tried not to sound hopeful but failed. I almost hated to dash her hopes. "Sergeant, do you want to answer Lynn's question?"

"Mrs. Quindt is *not* under arrest. We need her help so she's going to the station with me."

I thought I heard the disappointed hiss of her in-drawn breath and flashed her a smile. "Tell Uncle Barney where I am when he gets back."

When we were outside, Sergeant Griffin asked, "You want to take your car?"

"No, I'll walk back. It's just a few blocks." Seated in the squad car on our way to the station, I said, "You want to give me a hint what this is about?"

"Duchess. We got the autopsy report. Lieutenant Keller took one look at it and asked me to fetch you."

That gave me something to think about on the way to Sam's office. *What could be in that report that caused my cousin to send for me? And why would I know something about it?*

I didn't have to wait. Sam met me in front of his office door.

"Thanks for coming," he said and asked me to take a seat. He remained standing behind his desk. "What do you know about Duchess? Her real name? If she's got family? Anything?"

I shook my head. "We talked briefly but she never said anything about her past. What's in the autopsy report? How did she die?"

"She was poisoned."

I almost toppled off the chair. "What? That can't be right. Nobody else got sick from our food. I'm not even sure she was at the shelter. You've got to be mistaken..." I stared at Sam, horrified.

"You served enchiladas for dinner on Friday?"

"Yes. But they were vegetarian. My recipe. If they'd had a meat filling I could conceivably believe that—"

"It wasn't the enchiladas that were bad but what somebody added to them. To the serving she ate."

"What was added?"

"Ground castor beans."

I knew my mouth dropped open. I stared at him speechlessly. With an effort I pulled myself together. "Now I know you're wrong. Castor beans? How would anybody at the shelter get a hold of something that exotic?"

"They're not all that exotic. I was told they're used

for ornamental purposes. Arts and craft shops probably carry them."

"How did Duchess get a hold of them?" I asked, my mind still reeling.

"Somebody put them in her enchilada. The spices in the filling disguised their taste. Also, she had quite a bit of beer in her system, which undoubtedly dulled her senses."

"So the beans were cooked—"

"No. High heat destroys the ricin. That's the poison in the beans. They were ground in a blender or food processor or smashed with a rock and added to the regular beans and rice in the tortilla."

"I can't believe this. Why would somebody want to hurt Duchess? She was nice and certainly harmless. A poor, homeless, elderly woman."

"Just because she didn't have a home doesn't mean that the usual motives don't apply. Last year a homeless man was beaten half to death over the ownership of a pack of cigarettes."

"What if Duchess wasn't the intended victim?" I asked, thinking out loud. "Maybe the poisoner just wanted to get rid of one of the homeless and Duchess was at the wrong place at the wrong time?"

Sam snorted. "You know how crazy that sounds?"

He actually rolled his eyes. All the Kellers have blue eyes, including me, but while some of them, like Sam, my mother, and Uncle Barney inherited golden blond curls, some of us, like Maxi and I, got stuck with plain brown hair.

"You know there are people who'd like to see the shelter closed down. The location has become prime commercial real estate." When he didn't respond, I asked, "Can *you* come up with a motive?"

He shrugged. "You want to bet that it'll be something stupid, like a place next to the stove, or a cigarette, or a couple of snorts of hooch?"

"I would agree with you except this wasn't a spur of the moment act. As you pointed out, the beans had to be ground and somehow added to her food without her noticing it. And you can't buy the castor beans at the nearest convenience store. All this took planning."

Sam rubbed his chin thoughtfully. "You're right." He sat down and stared at the wall for a while. Then he roused himself. "Are you sure you don't know anything about Duchess? Think, Cybil."

I did. I shook my head. "She had a kitten she doted on. I found it and took it home."

"Aha! Maybe we need to interrogate the kitten."

Now it was my turn to roll my eyes. "This isn't a movie. She wasn't wearing a fancy collar studded with precious gems or secret messages sewn into the leather. She wasn't wearing any kind of collar. She's just a scrawny little thing who probably weighs three pounds sopping wet and has only one eye. Dr. Laura examined her. No secret microchips imbedded under her skin. Just a little stray in need of a home."

"Which you provided."

"Yes. So?"

"Don't get all defensive. But you are a soft touch. Stop denying that. What did Luke have to say about it?"

"Nothing. It's none of his business if I adopt a pet or not. And why should I not rescue one of God's creatures? My house is big enough, and I can afford to feed her."

"Don't get all bent out of shape, Cybil. It's a nice thing you did." He rose. "If you hear anything at the shelter let me know."

I said I would.

On my way out I remembered something. "Chico had a Biblical quotation in his pocket. Did Duchess?"

Sam glanced at a sheet of paper on his desk. "No."

"Not in her bag either?"

Sam looked at me with a frown. "What bag?"

"She always carried a carpetbag slung over her shoulder."

Sam called in Sergeant Griffin and asked him.

"No bag," the sergeant said. "Somebody must have snatched it before we found her body."

He was probably right. "Oh, and speaking of Chico. Did you check to see if he had a driver's license?"

"Not in Indiana. But that doesn't mean he never

had a license in another state. Or that he didn't know how to drive a car."

I nodded and left.

BY TEN THAT EVENING my kitchen was fragrant with vanilla, chocolate, cinnamon, and ginger. I'd washed the last of the cookie sheets and collapsed on a kitchen chair, a pot of herbal tea steaming in front of me. Tired but pleased, I looked at the trays of cookies I'd baked for the fund-raiser at the shelter. A good evening's work.

Buddy ate the bits of cookie dough I'd dropped on the floor. "You're better than a vacuum cleaner," I told her. She came to sit near my feet but not too close because she was still skittish. "You miss Duchess, don't you? You poor little thing. But this is your home now and nobody will make you leave."

She looked at me unblinking with her one golden eye.

I WAS TIDYING MY DESK the next day when my uncle used the intercom to summon me to his office.

Seeing Abby sitting in the visitor's chair I stopped, surprised.

"You two obviously know each other," Uncle Barney said. "Cybil, please sit down."

I did, looking questioningly at Abby. Though she seemed composed, her hands were tightly folded in her lap.

"Miss Sorensen has hired us to look into recent events at Mercy Shelter," he told me.

"There was another death," Abby said, her voice trembling.

"Who?"

"Mick. I don't know if you remember him. He always wore a gray cap with a brim, and if you listened carefully you could hear a hint of an Irish brogue in his voice. We asked him recently to be a helper in exchange for a bed."

"I remember him. What happened?"

"Last night one of the men came in and said Mick was sick. I went out back and called an ambulance right away. I followed the ambulance to the emergency room. Several hours later, Luke told me that Mick died."

"How?"

"Your husband thought he'd been poisoned. We'll know for sure after the autopsy."

"How awful," I said before I realized how inadequate my words were.

"People are afraid to come into the shelter. We actually had food left over this morning. You know that's never happened before," Abby said.

"But Duchess wasn't poisoned by our food, and I'm sure neither was Mick."

"That doesn't matter. Once the rumors get started—"

"So what can we do?" I asked, looking at Uncle Barney.

"For starters, you'll be at the shelter full-time. Your cover will be that you had some free time and decided to volunteer."

"Okay, but the men don't exactly confide in the staff," I pointed out.

"That's why Glenn, one of our investigators," Barney explained to Abby, "will pose as a homeless man and spend time at Mercy Shelter."

Poor Glenn. Even just pretending to be homeless for a few hours each day in this cold weather would be no picnic.

MY NEW SCHEDULE HAD me report to the shelter for breakfast one day and for dinner the next. I started with the dinner shift.

I made big pots of marinara sauce with ground beef in it which we would serve over penne. I tasted the sauce and added a half cup of dry basil to each pot to kick up the flavor.

Just before we opened the door for dinner, a distinguished-looking, late-fifty-something man, dressed in a three-piece suit, a designer tie, and highly polished shoes, joined me.

"I'm Frederick Holmes," he said, offering his hand.

I introduced myself and eyed him dubiously. He must have sensed my doubts and explained that he was a member of the Westport Men's Service Club, an organization of businessmen who did volunteer work in the community. My stepfather was a member of this group, I recalled.

Frederick rolled up the sleeves of his white shirt and grabbed a clean apron from the drawer. He had obviously been at the shelter before.

"I don't remember seeing you here," he said.

"That's because I usually work the breakfast shift."

"Ah." He obviously waited for me to elaborate.

"I'm between assignments, so I thought I'd lend a hand serving dinner."

"Assignments? What do you do?"

Uncle Barney and I had worked out a background story, replete with references should anyone check. "I'm a freelance writer. Mostly technical stuff."

The timer went off. I removed the loaves of garlic bread from the ovens. "You can help me slice this bread," I said. We worked side by side in silence for a while.

"What sort of technical stuff?" he asked.

"Most recently I wrote copy for a pharmaceutical company. They wanted a new brochure. Before that, I wrote for a company that makes kitty litter." This was sort of true, if truth could be less than absolute. Uncle Barney had me spend a day at both companies so that I could gain a superficial knowledge of what they did. Just enough to sound convincing. As we were coming dangerously close to the bottom of my knowledge I decided to go on the offensive.

"You said you belonged to a businessmen's group. What is your business?" I asked boldly.

"I own Classic Greens and Garden Services. You probably never paid any attention to our fertilizer factory but you may have noticed our greenhouses south of town."

I had noticed the unpleasant smell coming from the factory but decided not to comment on that. "I've been to your nursery. I don't know how many flats of petunias and marigolds I've bought there each spring."

He smiled, pleased. "I hope they did well for you."

"They certainly did." I glanced at my watch. "Time to start serving."

After dinner I stayed at the shelter to put up Christmas decorations. I couldn't bear to display my decorations at home, as they brought back too many memories of my sweet little boy and our last Christmas together. I'd held Ryan on my lap while he examined the exquisite figurines in the crèche. He had given each of the little carved animals a name. My throat closed with pain. I forced myself to take a couple of deep breaths.

When I had myself under control, I asked Pete to help me with the decorations. He must have noticed my agitation for he asked me if anything was wrong. Unable to speak, I shook my head and gave him half the evergreen branches I'd brought. We arranged them in two tall vases. Their fresh, green scent filled the air.

"We'll drape these garlands around the tall window," I told him. "Will you fetch the two stepladders from the storage room?"

Pete did and placed one on each side of the window. I climbed onto one ladder and, using huge thumbtacks, fastened the garlands to the wooden frame on my side. I looked at Pete. He'd tried to climb onto the other ladder but stopped on the second rung looking pale and shaky.

"What's wrong, Pete? You look sick."

"I can't," he said, his voice faint. "I can't climb any higher."

I saw beads of sweat on his forehead. "That's okay, Pete. Climb back down." I watched him step down gingerly, obviously relieved and a little embarrassed. This was the first time I'd actually seen someone in the throes of the fear of heights. The fear seemed real and terrifying.

"It's okay," I assured him and climbed up on the other ladder to finish the job.

"I'm sorry, Mrs. Quindt," he said softly.

"Don't worry about it. Look, it's done." I stepped back to look at the window. The garland looked festive. "All we have to do now is decorate the little tree on the table in the corner."

While he helped me, I asked in a conversational tone, "Were you here when Mick got sick?"

"Yes."

"Did you actually see him eat here?"

"I've thought about that. I know I saw him outside before dinner but I couldn't swear in a court of law that he ate here. When you live on the street one day is pretty much like another."

The uncomplaining resignation in his voice caused me to stare at him for a moment. I thought he looked as if he wanted to say something else. "What?" I asked encouragingly.

"Mick was always more interested in drinking than eating. I saw him frequently trade his food for a bottle of beer or a half pint of cheap vodka."

The poison could have been put into his liquor. Almost anyone could have made the trade. But why poison him?

Pete spoke. "I don't see how the poison could have been administered here at the shelter. We walk along the steam table where volunteers dish out the food. It's not as if we go through in a fixed order. It's first come, first served."

"I don't see how it could have been put into the food either. That leaves the vodka."

"No liquor's allowed inside the shelter so it had to have been put in somewhere in the neighborhood. Mick, like the rest of us who come to the shelter, don't have cars anymore. We don't wander off too far."

"Did Mick get into fights when he was drinking?"

Pete looked away.

I sensed his unease. "I know about the no-drinking and no-fighting rule in the shelter. I won't repeat anything you tell me unless it's directly relevant to his death."

"Mick did get into a few scrapes. They didn't amount to much because the men would break them up. Nobody wants to lose shelter privileges."

"Anyone in particular he had disagreements with?" Again Pete hesitated before he spoke.

"Earl. Chico's friend. But Earl doesn't get along with most of the men. He's mean and surly and Mick is…was hot-tempered. As I said, the fights weren't much except some pushing and shoving."

Unless Earl was the type who held a grudge and went in for retribution at a more opportune time. I'd ask Glenn to take a closer look at Earl.

"Did Mick and Duchess know each other?" I saw Pete's body go rigid. Was this something he'd already considered?

"They sometimes shared a bottle," he finally said.

So their deaths could be connected. They could have seen or overheard something, but what on earth could two homeless souls have witnessed that was significant or dangerous enough to get them killed?

We finished the decorating but I could scarcely look at the Christmas lights without feeling a deep sadness. How on earth was I going to get through Christmas?

Pete went out, and I locked the back door. When I unlocked my car I heard my name called softly.

"Over here, Cybil," Glenn said in a stage whisper.

To make my crossing to the other side of the car seem natural, I took the long-handled brush from my car and wiped off the thin layer of snow that covered the windows.

Glenn stayed in a crouch so that he was hidden by the car.

"Anything in particular I should be looking out for?" he asked.

"A guy named Earl. He had a fight with Mick. Be careful. Earl is mean and ill-tempered."

"I got a bottle of muscatel. Maybe that'll sweeten him up a little."

"Don't get him drunk. That might make him even meaner. And don't you drink anything. Just pretend. You need to keep your wits about you."

"Yes, mother," Glenn said, his voice a model of mock meekness and patient suffering.

"How long are you going to stay around here?"

"Several hours."

"Where did you park your car?"

"In the public library parking lot. There are a couple of ways I can get there from here without being spotted."

"You be careful. Two people have died. Three if we count Chico. So whatever is going on is serious. And the killer doesn't seem to be discriminating."

Glenn raised his arm in a half salute before he scooted around the parked van. I didn't see him again until he stood up near the fence. He must have duck-walked all the way there.

I DROVE HOME. ENTERING the kitchen I called Buddy. I didn't see her anywhere although her food dish was empty. I picked up the box of kitty chow and rattled it. From the corner of my eye I saw a slight movement on the bookcase that housed my collection of cookbooks.

"How did you get up there? You're so little." She showed me in reverse order. From the bookcase she jumped onto the counter, then the chair and from there to the floor. I fed her. Then I examined the fridge for people food. The only things I found were a couple of containers of leftovers. Since they came from Maxi's kitchen I knew they'd still taste good. I settled for a piece of fried chicken, Maxi's special slaw, and minted carrots.

Buddy sniffed the air and parked herself by my feet to watch me eat. I offered her a sliver of chicken which she gobbled down in record time. From then on it was one bite for me and one for her.

I had turned the library at the back of the house into my bedroom, saving me from having to heat the entire upstairs. I didn't mind sleeping surrounded by books, and the room's vicinity to the bathroom more than made up for its small closet. The previous owner had converted a wood-burning fireplace into a gas-burning one which I turned on, more for the beauty of the flames than the actual heat.

After my shower I sat by the fire and read. Maxi had given me a copy of the Austrian author who'd been awarded the Nobel Prize for Literature, and though the novel was beautifully written, it was very dark. The mother-daughter relationship it depicted was an odd mixture of codependency and emotional tug-of-war for domination. With the recent deaths at the shelter, I wasn't in the mood for anything quite this noir. Safer to reread a Jane Austen where the relational and familial bloodletting was a lot less dark and far more elegant.

The rhythm of the crackling of the flames was suddenly accompanied by a soft, high sound. It took me several seconds before I identified the source. I opened my bedroom door and in streaked an orange bundle of fur. Before I even reached the bed, Buddy had jumped up on it and proceeded to investigate the quilt. I slipped into bed and watched her. After a while she settled down next to my knees. Her purring was oddly comforting and her small body pleasantly warm.

I MET WITH UNCLE BARNEY to report that I had essentially nothing to report. I finished by saying that I didn't think the killer was one of the homeless.

"I agree with Cybil," Glenn said, scratching his unshaven chin.

I moved my chair a little away from him. "No offense, Glenn, but your eau de cologne is a little—"

"Ripe?" he asked, grinning and fingering his moth-eaten sweater.

"Decidedly ripe." He didn't seem to mind his unhygienic, aromatic state.

"Why isn't the killer one of the homeless?" Barney wanted to know, clamping his unlit pipe between his teeth.

"Because of the way the victims were killed," I said. "Too complicated."

Glenn nodded. "Having spent three days among the homeless, I'm guessing that if the killer were one of them, he would be more…direct. You know, a good whack over the head with a rock or a brick. Maybe a knife between the ribs, but not poison."

"And if poison," I added, "then it would be something that you can buy anywhere, like rat poison, not something you'd have to go to a special store for. The homeless wouldn't know where such a store was, and they don't walk around with a pocketful of money."

"And when they do have money they wouldn't spend it on castor beans," Glenn said. "My muscatel was a big hit. So are cigarettes and candy bars. Shoes that don't have holes in them. Warm socks. Mittens. And the ultimate luxury: a room of their own."

"Shades of Virginia Woolf," I murmured.

"What?" Glenn asked.

I shook my head. "Nothing." Then I thought of all the promises made during the recent city elections and my anger rose. "And what is his honor, our mayor, doing about the homeless, except ordering the cops to hassle them? I get so angry—"

"Cybil, that's a discussion for another time. Right now our problem is to stop whoever is killing them. If we don't, the other problem could become academic."

My breath caught. "Uncle Barney, you think there might be more murders?"

He tapped the stem of his pipe against his teeth. "I don't know for sure but something about this case is just off enough to make me think there might be."

"I agree," Glenn said. "Don't get me wrong. Most of these men aren't exactly models of mental and emotional stability, but I can't see them plotting cold-blooded murders. That's out of their league."

I decided to voice my opinion out loud. That was the nice thing about our discussions. Uncle Barney didn't mind if we speculated out loud, and he never scoffed at our ideas no matter how far out they were. "Worst-case scenario—a serial killer is targeting the homeless. How can we possibly catch someone like that?" I asked.

"Sooner or later the murderer will make a mistake and then another, and we'll get a lead. Then we'll ask the Westport PD for help," he said.

"And what are the chances that they'll help us?" Glenn asked.

"We'll worry about that when the time comes."

Uncle Barney was good about not borrowing trouble. As he always told me, trouble comes sooner or later so there's no need to go looking for it. He was right, of course, but somehow I could not adopt this attitude. Much of my life was spent wondering and fretting over what-if scenarios.

"Have you gotten close to any clients at the shelter?" Barney asked.

I nodded. "Pete. I'm pretty sure Abby will make him one of the monitors who gets a permanent bed in the dormitory. He strikes me as an educated man. I wish I could ask him about his previous life."

"I'll see what I can find out tonight," Glenn offered. "And don't worry. I'll be casual and tactful."

I kept myself from flicking him a disbelieving look. Subtlety and tact weren't Glenn's strong points.

WHILE THE CHICKEN STEW we would be serving for supper was simmering on the stove, I decided to look for Duchess's bag. It had to be somewhere in the neighborhood. I'd kept a sharp eye out for it but had not seen anyone with it in the shelter. My guess was that whoever took it emptied it and discarded it somewhere in the area.

I opened the dumpsters behind the shelter. They had been emptied recently. The good thing about that was that I didn't have to dig through them; the bad thing was that the bag could be in the city dump, buried under tons of garbage.

If I were a homeless person, would I take a chance to come to the shelter and throw a bag into the dumpster after I took its contents? No. I'd discard it quickly. Stuff it behind or under something. With that in mind, I circled the four blocks nearest the shelter. When I came to the house where I'd found the kitten I decided to search the yard.

There wasn't much to search. The hulk of an old pickup. With its door ripped off it didn't provide much of a hiding place. I went to the spot from where I'd retrieved the kitten. Lying face down in the snow, I shone the beam from the flashlight under the house. Though the light wasn't all that strong I did see something to my left. I couldn't reach it. I got up and looked for a stick. A recently fallen branch enabled me to drag the item close enough to grab it.

Eureka!

I opened the bag. It was empty except for a small

piece of paper that had been jammed into one of its side pockets. Carefully I unfolded it.

"The day of the Lord so cometh as a thief in the night."

FOUR

"THIS QUOTE IS FROM Thessalonians," Maxi said, studying the piece of paper I had found in Duchess's bag. "I'm sure of it." She handed it back to me.

We looked at each other. "You think it's possible that some religious nut is killing homeless people?" I shook my head at my own preposterous thought. "That would make no sense. If you go around quoting the Bible, you wouldn't go around killing people."

"If you're sane, you wouldn't. But Cybil, do you really think we're dealing with a sane person here?"

Shivering, I said, "You know how scary that idea is?"

"Yes, and that's why I want you to park right by the back door and leave as soon as dinner is over. Better yet, walk to your car with someone you trust. Or phone Luke to meet you."

"I'm not phoning Luke. That would only provide him with extra fodder for his claims that my current lifestyle is inappropriate or irresponsible or whatever he's labeling it today."

"All right. I'll ask Barney to meet you. Or to send one of his men."

I opened my mouth to protest but when my grandmother had that look on her face you might as well argue with a tree stump for all the good it would do you. "Glenn's here. I'll ask him to stick around the parking lot until I drive off."

Maxi nodded, satisfied. "We'll have to give this paper to the police. It's evidence and they're in a better position to trace it."

We finished setting out the cookies for the fund-raising sale on several tables we'd pushed together. On the other side of the room, tables featured all sorts of decorative items. Having very limited talents in the area of arts and crafts, I admired the contributions we had received. I had my eye on a pretty basket. It would be perfect for my kitchen table. I could keep my supply of fresh fruit in it.

I had sent invitations to all the movers and shakers of Westport as well as posted notices of the event on the bulletin boards of grocery stores and the community center. A *Westport Gazette* reporter had written a brief but nice article about the sale. Maxi and I expected a good turnout.

We weren't disappointed. Maxi manned the cash register at the end of the cookie table and I the one at the arts and crafts display. The cookies sold out in record time, and I had only a few items left on my table.

Frederick Holmes, one of our regular volunteers, came with his wife and helped Maxi for a while.

"We did well," Maxi announced after counting the money.

The door opened. I turned, ready to tell the late-comer that we were closed when I saw that it was Luke.

"You're too late. The cookies are all gone," I told him.

"No, they're not. I saved a nice selection for you," Maxi said with a smile. She pulled one of those white bakery boxes from under the table.

I should have anticipated that.

"Maxi, you're the sweetest woman in the whole world," Luke said and kissed her cheek.

He also handed her two twenty dollar bills. Expensive cookies, I thought, but since it was for the shelter, I kept my mouth shut. Besides, we no longer shared a join bank account so I had no right to voice my opinion on how he spent his money.

Luke sauntered over to my tables and looked at what was left. "Tell you what," he said. "I'll take these three, whatever they are." He pointed to the small sleighs filled with holly featuring a thick, red candle.

"Centerpieces. What are you going to do with three?" I asked, mentally picturing his small apartment.

"The girls in the office will like these, don't you think?"

"Yes," I said and placed the sleighs into a bag before he could change his mind.

Luke paid Maxi and then walked her to her car. He came back to do the same for me.

"That isn't necessary," I told him. "Glenn is somewhere outside."

"Yeah, I saw him. Gave him some of my cookies."

"That was nice of you."

"I *am* generally a nice guy, which is probably part of my problem with you."

"And how do you figure that?"

"If I were a less easygoing husband, I'd never have let you move out and given you the space and time you insist you need."

"I have news for you. Bullying me wouldn't have worked at all."

Luke smiled a little ruefully. "I know it wouldn't have. Ready to leave?"

"As soon as I lock up the cash and the checks in the office."

"YOU WANT TO TASTE the chili?" I asked Abby the next evening.

"Sure."

I ladled some into a bowl and handed it to her. "Careful, it just stopped bubbling."

She blew on her spoon before she tasted the chili. She nodded. "It's good. Personally I'd like it a little hotter…"

"Me too, but when you cook for a crowd you have to err on the side of mild. If you help me fill these glass shakers with hot pepper flakes, we can get them on the tables before Pete opens the door to our volunteer servers." When he did, I noticed that Frederick, nattily dressed in a dark blue suit, was among them.

"What do you know about Frederick Holmes?" I asked Abby.

She glanced at him and then at me. "Not much except he's one of our more civic-minded business owners. Why?"

I shrugged. "There's something about him. I can't put my finger on what it is..."

"Maybe he's a little too good?"

"Yes, maybe. Makes you wonder why he's trying so hard. What he's atoning for." I shook my head. "Maybe I'm getting a little jaded."

"I don't think so. As we get older we don't accept so many things at face value anymore."

"I've never been able to decide whether that's good or bad."

"It's neither. It's inevitable. Experience teaches us to be a little skeptical," Abby said.

The long line of hungry men approaching us ended our discussion.

I SLIPPED INTO MY good little black dress which I had dry-cleaned especially for dinner at my mother's house. If I didn't dress up she'd be disappointed and feel that she'd totally failed to instill a fashion sense in me. I knew that my choice of profession was a disappointment to her as was my separation from Luke. So to feel less guilty for falling short of her expectations, I accepted her dinner invitation.

Not that the food wouldn't be good. It would be excellent, as my mother had hired a first-rate chef after marrying Justin Merriweather, her fourth husband—or was it technically her third since she'd married her second husband twice? I've never been clear on that.

What would not be enjoyable was the formal atmosphere, my stepfather's somewhat fussy manner and pompous attitude, and possibly the guests, depending on whether they were from my mother's A-list or B-list or family members. I was hoping hard they'd be family members as I had murders on my mind and didn't feel up to making tons of small talk. Plus I think I was coming down with a cold.

For a touch of color, I added the turquoise necklace Luke had given me for our fourth wedding anniversary. We had still been a happy family then. Quickly I dismissed the memories and drove to my mother's house.

I saw Luke right after my mother opened the door. Was she matchmaking? Maybe, though she liked Luke enough to invite him just to see him.

"You look great, Mom. New dress?" To her credit

she didn't simper and murmur something like "This old thing?" but acknowledged that she had been shopping in Chicago earlier in the week. Knowing her shopping habits and tastes, it must have cost Justin a small fortune. Good thing he could afford it.

Mom introduced me to her other guests, which included Frederick Holmes and his wife, Brittany, who is closer to my age than his. Groomed, bejeweled, and made up to within an inch of her life, Brittany was attractive but seemed a little ill at ease. Did she feel out of place?

Before dinner, she was sitting on the love seat in the alcove. I joined her.

"Brittany, do you have children?" I asked.

"Two stepsons, Tyler and Cameron, Frederick's sons from his first marriage."

"So they're grown up?"

"Yes, supposedly, but they seem to live at our house more than anywhere else."

For a moment her expression suggested that she didn't like them being around that much but she quickly masked her emotion with a small smile.

"Adult children moving in and out of their parents' houses seems to be the trend of the time," I said. "It's expensive, setting up a household of their own."

"Some seem to take a lot longer than others to get settled," she said with a trace of resentment. "Of course, it's so much easier to come home to crash, get a free meal, clean laundry, and mooch money off of dear old dad."

I didn't say anything. Luke claimed my silences were an invitation for others to talk.

"Cameron—he's the older son—has a severe eating problem. Frederick disagrees with me that we ought to take him for special counseling. It's unhealthy to be so heavy, especially for someone his age. And Tyler smokes like a chimney. Also a healthy habit," she said with undisguised sarcasm, "but Frederick says Tyler will quit when he's ready. Ha!"

Obviously the couple didn't see eye to eye about the two young men.

Frederick came to escort us to the dinner table. He had been talking to my stepfather but had been watching us from across the room. I had the impression he was wondering about, maybe even worrying about, the topic of our conversation.

Sitting across from me, he said, "Isn't it awful about the murders at the shelter?"

"I was never crazy about Cybil volunteering there and now it could be downright dangerous," Elizabeth said.

My mother looked at me as disapprovingly as if I'd worn an outfit featuring plaids, stripes, polka dots, and fat cabbage roses. "Mom, murder can happen anywhere, even at the fanciest mansion in town," I said. I watched to see if she got my reference to the murder of Terrance Ariosto which happened when

I first started to work at the agency. By the slightly uncomfortable look on her face I knew she did.

"But there it was a family matter," she said, "while here it's sheer brutality bred by animal survival."

Luke, who sat on my right, placed his hand over mine in a soothing manner but I wasn't in the mood to be soothed. "Are you suggesting murder is more acceptable if it is based on greed rather than on the need to survive? Seems to me it's the other way around."

"Murder is wrong no matter what the reason for it is," Maxi said, her voice forceful enough to close the subject.

It didn't.

"If I had my way, we'd round up the homeless each morning to take them to work sites. That way they could support themselves," Frederick announced, and my stepfather agreed heartily.

"Yes, make them work." Elizabeth seconded the idea with a nod.

This from a woman who hadn't been gainfully employed a single day in her life.

"Take them off the street," she added. "It's embarrassing when we have guests on football weekends and have to drive through downtown past these people. They're so dirty and scruffy."

My mother shuddered delicately while anger surged through me strong enough to make speech impossible for a moment. Luke took my hand in his. My free hand crumpled the napkin in my lap so forcefully that it probably left permanent creases in the linen.

"Why Mom, you surprise me. I didn't think you even saw them." As always, irony was wasted on her.

"It's hard to miss them, the way they stand around and gawk at people driving by," she said.

"Maybe they gawk at you and your car in envy, thinking that if they had jobs they could also have what you have." Luke pressed my hand. A warning, I thought.

"Exactly. Give them work and they can get off the street," Frederick agreed enthusiastically.

"On minimum wage?" I asked. Maxi and I exchanged a look that plainly asked in what la-la land did these people live?

"Well, this discussion could be academic anyway," Frederick said, his voice mysterious and a little smug.

"Why?" Maxi asked.

"The shelter may be closed soon and sold."

I knew both Maxi and I held our breath for a beat. "Where did you hear that?" I asked.

"It was mentioned at the last city council meeting, wasn't it, Justin?" Frederick asked.

Justin nodded. "The topic came up."

"Well, it can be discussed from now till doomsday by a bunch of old men, but that doesn't mean it'll happen," Maxi said, looking at her son-in-law severely.

"Who wants to buy the shelter?" I asked. Frederick hesitated, but the need to be the center of attention was too strong.

"Several businessmen are interested. The shelter sits on a prime piece of real estate."

"That's vague," I said, dismissing the threat to the shelter. Just to be sure, I asked, "Is there anyone specifically who wants the shelter?"

Frederick's small eyes lit up with what Maxi called *Schadenfreude*. There is no good translation for the word but it roughly means rejoicing over another's misfortunes. Maxi considers it one of the most ugly emotions humans are capable of—almost as bad as greed. I thought it was meaner and uglier.

"Who?" I repeated.

"Edgar Lee, for one."

"The owner of the Aces High Club? Why does he want it?" I asked, puzzled.

"To expand. I guess his gentlemen's club is so successful he needs a bigger place."

"What's a gentlemen's club?" Elizabeth asked.

"A sleazy strip joint," I answered before someone could give her a sanitized definition.

"Oh," Elizabeth murmured distastefully.

"You said the Aces High Club for one. Who else?" Maxi asked.

"The Reverend Brown needs a better location."

"Brimstone Brown? Are you serious?" I asked.

"Who's Brimstone Brown?" Luke wanted to know.

"That hellfire and brimstone preacher who has a Sunday morning show on the local television station," Maxi explained.

Frederick nodded. "I guess you can scare people into giving money if they think it'll help wipe out the bad they've done."

"The selling of absolution worked for a while in the sixteenth century but then backfired and caused the Reformation," Maxi said.

"Leave it to a librarian to have that kind of information at her fingertips," I said and smiled at Maxi, who smiled back at me. Luke stood up.

"Cybil, you said you had to go to work early, didn't you?" Luke asked, giving me a meaningful look.

"Yes. And I'm coming down with a cold. I need to go to bed. Thank you for dinner, Mom, it was excellent as always but we have to go."

"Don't you want dessert?" Elizabeth asked. "It's crème brûlée, your favorite."

"No, thank you. I'm trying to cut down on sugar." I leaned forward and kissed her on the cheek. Luke did the same.

"We can let ourselves out," I said. "You all stay seated and enjoy dessert."

When we reached the street, I said, "Thanks for

getting me out of there. I was heading for a major argument. Except you can't argue with someone like Mom who refuses to acknowledge anything that's unpleasant and displeasing. I love her, but her stance on social issues drives me crazy." I thought over what had been said. "What surprises me is Frederick's attitude. He volunteers at the shelter yet he so clearly dislikes and disapproves of his clients. That doesn't make any sense."

"No, it doesn't, but people aren't always logical," Luke reminded me, walking me to my car. He stopped to look at me. "Are you really coming down with a cold?"

"Yes. My throat is scratchy and my head feels like it's going to explode."

"I'll follow you to your house and make you some herbal tea."

"Is that the best the vaunted medical profession can come up with? Herbal tea?" I couldn't help teasing him a little.

"Yup. Herbal tea with honey and lemon and a vitamin C pill. And plenty of rest."

"That's pitiful. And you forgot to mention the two aspirin and that I'm supposed to call you in the morning." Luke grinned at me as he opened my car door.

On the way home I started to sneeze and my eyes watered so that I had trouble seeing. Good thing

Luke volunteered for tea duty because I didn't feel up to brewing a pot.

At the house he told me to put on my nightie. I did, then I wrapped myself in the soft chenille throw Maxi had given me and sat by the fire. My little orange cat sat at my feet.

Luke brought the tea. "Do you need anything else?"

"No, thank you." I used the mug to warm my hands while I waited for the tea to cool down a little. He bent down and patted Buddy's head. I'd have to teach him how to pet a cat properly.

"Do you want me to stay the night?" Luke asked.

I shook my head. "It's just a cold. You better go before you catch it."

"You know I never catch a cold."

He sounded a little self-satisfied which bugged me. "If you're going to gloat you may as well leave."

"Don't you want to hear what I found out about the poisonings at the shelter?"

That got my attention. "What did you find out?"

He sat in the other chair beside the fire. Buddy edged toward him. "Something in the autopsy report struck me as odd."

I waited.

"Do your clients have ready access to a blender?"

"A kitchen blender?" I asked, wondering where he was going with that question.

Luke nodded.

"We have one at the shelter but the kitchen is locked unless one of the regular volunteers or a staff member is there."

"So it would be difficult for a client to use a blender to grind castor beans?"

"Yes. Unless he somehow got into the kitchen when no one was around." I considered that for a moment. "But that's unlikely. After the break-in a few months ago, we had all the old locks replaced with new ones that Sam recommended as virtually burglar-proof."

"Where do the homeless keep their possessions?"

"Most have very few possessions and those they carry with them. At night we have footlockers in the dormitory that can be locked."

Luke stared into the fire for a long time. Absent-mindedly he stroked the silken fur of Buddy, who had inched closer to him.

That little ingrate. It had taken a lot longer for her to come that close to me, and I had saved her life. Ignoring my resentment, I said, "Sam hasn't made any progress in solving the murders."

"He probably needs a few more facts and clues."

I nodded. "All we know is that the poison used was castor beans administered in food. We have no idea what the motive might have been. None of the victims had anything worth getting killed for. And what on earth could they have known that posed a threat to anyone? Their world is a six-block area of a relatively rundown section of Westport. This makes no sense." I sighed deeply.

"Murder doesn't make sense except maybe to the murderer," Luke said.

We chatted a few more minutes before Luke went home.

PRIOR TO RESTOCKING the pantry with our Christmas bazaar earnings, I took inventory of what supplies we had on hand.

The shelter was quiet. The kitchen and dining room had been cleaned after supper and the lights turned off. The men had left: Those lucky enough to have gotten a bed for the night for the dormitory and the unlucky ones for their favorite doorway, bus shelter or other dry spot they had discovered in the neighborhood.

It had been a long, physically demanding day and I was tired. I carried a chair into the pantry so I could sit down while I tallied the food items on the shelves. We would definitely need canned tomatoes and beans. While I calculated how much we would save by buying dry beans rather than canned, I heard a noise.

I listened, holding my breath. When it remained quiet I decided I must have imagined it. Or mice had gotten into the building. In that case, I'd bring Buddy with me and let her loose. I had no idea if she knew how to catch a mouse, didn't know if that skill was instinctive or had to be taught by the mother cat.

Then I heard the noise again, coming from the back door. Someone was trying to get in? Why? The plaque beneath the overhead light instructed everyone to go to the front entrance.

The pantry had no windows, so to someone outside, this part of the building would look dark and appear to be deserted. But what could an intruder want from a shelter for the homeless? Surely they'd know that no money was kept on the premises. Nor would there be anything that could be fenced or sold easily. Could it be someone so hungry that they'd break in for food? If so I had to feed them.

Something kept me from turning on the kitchen lights. Though the Venetian blinds covered the windows, they let in enough light from the parking lot that I could see. I approached the back door as quietly as I could. The upper half of the door consisted of a window with a wrought iron grate over the glass. Not the most sturdy of doors and Abby kept talking about replacing it but money was always tight.

Before I reached the door I saw the outline of a shape through the window and stopped in my tracks. By the size of the dark shape it had to be a man. A large man. Tall with wide shoulders and a large head. Why didn't he knock or ring the bell? There was something stealthy in his stance. Could he see me? I was wearing dark gray slacks and a black cardigan over a dark gray blouse. As long as I didn't move quickly, I was probably safely hidden in the darkness of the room.

He rattled the doorknob again. Fear shot through me. The door wasn't strong but he appeared to be. As quickly as I could move without making a noise, I made my way to the telephone. Before I reached it, the door frame splintered.

"I called the cops. They're on their way," I said loudly and as convincingly as I could. "You better get out of here or spend the night in county jail."

I had backed up to the kitchen counter. Reaching behind me I grabbed the rolling pin. Made of marble, it could shatter bones if swung forcefully. The man apparently believed my threat and ran off. My knees felt weak. I needed to lean against the counter. That's how Glenn found me when he burst through the door and flipped on the light.

FIVE

"WHAT DO YOU SUPPOSE the intruder was after?" I asked Glenn when we were sitting in the kitchen. He had poured me a glass of milk and insisted I drink it to calm down. He watched to make sure that I did. I wasn't sure I could keep it down.

"My guess is that it was a simple burglary. He was hoping to find something in here he could trade for a bottle of hooch or cigarettes or drugs," Glenn said.

"In this kitchen?" I asked, looking around doubtfully.

"Sure. That percolator is nice. So's the toaster, the blender—"

"The blender," I murmured, remembering my conversation with Sam. "The police believe the castor beans used in the poisonings were ground in a blender."

"Did you ever find remnants of something in the blender?"

"No. It's always been clean and exactly where I put it." I shook my head. "I have a hard time believing that one of our men used it."

"Me too. That's too complicated. Our clients go

for the direct and the simple." Glenn thought for a moment. "Describe the intruder one more time."

I barely repressed a groan, having done so twice already: Once to him and once to Sergeant Griffin who'd arrived in response to Glenn's phone call. "He was big. Really big. He practically filled the doorway. From the way he moved, he had to be fairly young. He was wearing a dark-colored parka, jeans, and boots that laced up the front. As I told you, he wore a ski mask so I have no idea what his face looks like."

"The description doesn't fit anyone around here I know," Glenn said.

"I'm sure he isn't one of our regular clients."

"And he didn't say anything? You're sure?"

"I'm sure. He just stood there. Maybe that's what made him so menacing. And the ski mask." I shuddered, remembering.

"Well, it was cold, so that could have been the reason for the mask," Glenn said.

I could tell he didn't really believe this either. Though it was cold, the temperature wasn't arctic.

Sergeant Griffin returned. "I looked around outside, but there are so many footprints that it's impossible to tell which one belongs to the intruder."

"I looked, too, after Cybil told me what happened. He must have ducked into one of the buildings or got away through the alley," Glenn said, his tone apologetic.

The sergeant nodded and examined the door frame.

Glenn turned to me. "You better get a new door tomorrow. For tonight I'll nail a couple of boards across it."

"Okay," I said, hoping we'd have enough money to get a good, sturdy door.

"You're sure he wore gloves?" the sergeant asked.

"Or mittens. But everyone wears gloves or mittens in this weather."

"True, so there won't be any fingerprints on the door, but we'll check tomorrow anyway."

"We'll probably never know who he was," I said, discouraged, and the sergeant didn't disagree with me.

"Do you need Cybil for anything else?" Glenn asked.

"No. I think we're done for tonight. I'll stop by first thing in the morning to look around just in case we missed something in the dark. Good night."

"Thank you for coming so quickly," I called after him. "Good night."

Glenn got two boards and tools from the shed to secure the ruined kitchen door. I watched him, huddled inside my parka. When he finished, he asked, "You ready to leave? I'll walk you to your car."

"Thanks." I wanted to say that this wasn't necessary but couldn't. I was spooked. The slightest noise made me jump.

All the way home the big, dark, menacing shape of the man flashed through my mind. Part of me wanted to turn my car around and head for Maxi's farm where I'd be fussed over and where I'd feel safe. Or I could seek refuge in Luke's apartment. No, that wasn't an option unless I wanted to start a whole new set of problems. Taking a deep breath, I reminded myself that I was a grown woman who wasn't afraid of the dark. At least most of the time I wasn't.

After I parked my car in front of my house, I made a mad dash inside. I put the chain on and propped a chair under the doorknob of both the front and the back door. I also pulled the drapes shut on every single window, something I'd never done before.

Buddy followed me from room to room. "Tonight you better get into attack mode," I told her. Buddy was feisty and the look she gave me from her one tawny eye said that nobody had better mess with us or they'd be sorry.

ALL DAY I THOUGHT ABOUT Frederick's claim that both Edgar Lee of the Aces High Club and Preacher Brimstone Brown were interested in acquiring the shelter. The building was owned by the city, and since the council was facing a budget shortfall for the next calendar year I wouldn't put it past them to sell the building. It was already early December and close to the end of the budget year so there was no time to waste.

Glancing at my watch, I discovered it was already 3:30. The tall pots of vegetable soup were simmering nicely and could be left unattended for a while. The ham and cheese sandwiches were assembled, waiting to be grilled. I had no excuse for not visiting the bar and the church.

I put on my outdoor gear and the lovely mauve scarf Maxi had knitted for me. Just as I was thinking of her she walked in.

"Oma, it's good to see you," I said and kissed her on the cheek.

"I thought you might need help with supper." Noting that I was dressed for the outdoors, she asked, "Where are you going?"

"Remember our dinner conversation at Mom's house?" I watched Maxi roll her bright blue eyes. "I'm going to find out how seriously interested in buying the shelter the two parties are."

"If you're going to that strip club I'm going with you. I've never been to one of those."

"I haven't either. Let's go."

THE DOOR OF THE ACES High Club stood open, though the neon sign, featuring a top hat and the ace of hearts, wasn't turned on yet. Perhaps only the cleaning crew would be here this early but, having come, we both took deep breaths and decided to go in anyway.

Even with the door open and all the lights turned

on, except those on the small stage, it was dim inside. The smell was something else. The mixture of old cigarette smoke, various colognes and aftershave lotions, and stale beer made me want to hold my nose.

"Breathe through your mouth and you won't notice the smell as much," Maxi whispered. "They should open some windows."

"There aren't any," I whispered back and wondered why we felt we had to keep our voices down. "The windows are bricked shut."

"What on earth for?"

I shrugged. "Security? Privacy? They want people to come inside to watch and pay the cover charge?" In tandem we took a few more steps into the club. Standing shoulder to shoulder we looked around.

The small stage was in front of us. The bar ran along the left wall. The rest of the space was taken up with some tables and chairs. I could see why the owner wanted a bigger area.

"We're not open yet. What do you want?"

We both jumped at the voice behind us. From his high, boyish voice, I expected a small, slender man. The hulking figure approaching us made us both take a step back.

"We're here to see Mr. Lee," I said, trying not to sound intimidated.

"You got an appointment?"

"No, we didn't know we needed one," Maxi said.

"Well, you do."

"It's okay," a man said, stepping down from the dark stage, his voice friendlier than the young giant's.

"Mr. Lee?" I asked. When he nodded I introduced Maxi and myself.

"You're the ladies who run the shelter down the street."

"Some of them," Maxi said modestly.

"What can I do for you? Are you here to collect for the shelter? I give to the annual campaign and that's it."

"We're not collecting. You're aware of the homeless people who've been killed recently?" I asked.

"Yes. It's been all over the news. What a terrible thing."

I studied his face, trying to see if he was sincere but his smooth expression told me nothing. Slender, dark-haired with a thin black mustache, and impeccably dressed in a dark suit, he reminded me of the nightclub owners so commonly found in the noir films of the thirties and forties. I half expected to see Bette Davis or Barbara Stanwyck stroll in.

"I saw the cops around the shelter. Do they have any suspects?" he asked.

"If they do they didn't tell us," Maxi said. "Is it true that you're interested in buying the shelter?"

Edgar Lee leveled dark eyes on Maxi, eyes that revealed no emotions. "I might be interested. I could use a larger space. But that's not what you're asking, is it? You want to know if I'd do something to discredit the shelter and force it to close."

"How astute of you and yes, that's what we're asking," Maxi admitted.

"You have a lot of nerve. I would not commit murder no matter how much I wanted the building. In this state they execute you for murder."

"Yes, they do," Maxi agreed. "Any guesses who'd do such a thing?"

"No." He hesitated. "I don't want to accuse anyone but I'm not the only one interested in buying the building."

"Who else is interested?" I asked.

"That nutjob preacher on the next block."

Frederick's information had been correct. I wondered where he'd gotten it.

The lights on the stage flicked on and a woman stepped to the front.

"It's freezing cold in here," she complained.

I stared at her. The sheer dressing gown she wore was open, revealing what had to be a G-string and a tiny, tiny bra with tassels on it. No wonder she was cold. I shivered just looking at her goosebump-covered flesh.

"I can't rehearse in this cold," she said.

"You can. Put the music on and move. You'll get warm fast enough," Lee snapped without sympathy. He turned to us. "Ladies, you'll have to excuse me. My other dancers will be here any minute with a dozen complaints and problems before they rehearse."

"They rehearse?" Maxi asked.

"Exotic dancing isn't as easy as most people think. It's an art. You ever see a good strip show?"

We both shook our heads.

"Come in some night. I'll leave word at the door to let you in for free. Our first show's at ten. I think you'll be pleasantly surprised."

"You're sure you know nothing about the murders?" I asked.

"I don't. Good-bye, ladies."

So dismissed, we left.

Outside Maxi asked, "Should we be scandalized by his invitation to see a show some evening?"

"Probably. Still, I'm a little curious. Aren't you?" We looked at each other furtively.

"But let's not forget that curiosity killed the cat," Maxi said.

NEXT WE HEADED TO THE Church of Holiness. The sign out front listed the Reverend Eli Brown as minister.

"I didn't know Brimstone's first name was Eli," I said.

"His mother would hardly have named him Brimstone," Maxi said, her voice mildly reproving.

"No, I guess not."

Reverend Brown was the opposite in appearance

to the club owner. Where the latter had been neat and elegantly dressed, the preacher looked like Hollywood's version of someone from the Old Testament. He wore a caftanlike robe made of some rough material that once might have been feed sacks. Suspended from the rope around his waist was a silver cross. It was his beard and haircut, however, that drew my gaze. The beard was gray-streaked and reached to his chest while his hair looked as if someone had put a small bowl on his head and cut the hair around it. I concentrated on his face. I looked into his eyes and all but recoiled from the intensity of his gaze. Not a man to cross. I blinked. When I looked at him again, his expression had changed to a benign mildness.

"My secretary said you wanted to see me?"

His voice—low, pleasing, resonant—could hold an audience. Maybe even mesmerize it or whip it into a frenzy.

After introductions, I told him what our visit was about.

"Sisters, we are in the same business," he said.

"How's that, reverend?" Maxi asked.

"Call me Brother Eli. Reverend is too formal. You see, you take care of the physical needs of the homeless and I of their spiritual needs."

"Are you having any success?" Maxi asked skeptically.

"Some. Not as much as you. People always see to their physical needs first."

"It's hard to think of your soul when your stomach is grumbling with hunger," Maxi said with an impatient flick of her hand.

My grandmother's tone had turned impatient if not downright acerbic, and it was time for me to take over if we were to get any information from him. "Brother Eli, each of the victims had a piece of paper with a quotation from the Bible on it. Did they get those quotes here?"

"The police asked me the same question."

"And what was your answer?"

"Not from me, strictly speaking."

"But you know where they got them?"

"Yes. A member of my flock who is…let's just call him a lay preacher, for lack of a better term. He distributes these outside the church on most Sunday mornings. The people in the neighborhood call him the Maniac Messiah. I try to get them to stop calling him that, but without success."

"Why do they call him that?" I asked.

"If you ever heard him, you'd understand. Now will you excuse me, sisters—"

"One more thing. Was Duchess a member of your flock?"

"She'd come occasionally." He shrugged. "She came whenever I told her there would be cookies and coffee after the service. A little bribery"—he shrugged again—"but for a good cause."

"What is the Maniac Messiah's real name?" Maxi asked.

"Calvin Laxton."

"Where does this Calvin Laxton live?"

Brother Eli lowered his gaze and studied his hands. "I'm never quite sure. He moves around a lot."

"But he's here most Sundays?" I asked.

"Yes. Sisters, you must excuse me now."

He preceded us to the door and opened it. "Why don't you stop by some Sunday morning? Our service starts at ten."

"Thank you," Maxi murmured.

"Bless you, sisters."

Finding ourselves outside, I said, "He certainly gave us the bum's rush. I think the good brother was lying about not knowing where this Maniac Messiah is."

"I had that impression too."

"What did you think of Edgar Lee?" I asked.

"I'm not sure. If he lied he did it very well."

"Yes. He was smooth." Something about the man bothered me. A little too smooth?

We headed back to the shelter where we finished preparing the evening meal.

AFTER DINNER I WENT TO see Uncle Barney at the agency. Everyone else had gone home so for once I escaped Lynn's usual interrogation. I heaved a sigh of relief.

Since I wasn't sure how my uncle felt about Lynn, I was careful not to make any disparaging remarks about her or to let him know that I didn't much like the woman. I passed her desk quickly and went into my uncle's office.

"Uncle Barney, I'm wasting my time and the agency's money at the shelter," I wailed before I dropped into a chair.

"Tired?" he asked in sympathy.

"Exhausted. It's one thing to volunteer a day at the shelter and another being there all day, every day, and cooking two meals." I sighed. "But I wouldn't mind if I got some sort of results."

"Glenn told me about the attempted break-in."

"Wasn't that odd? What could the intruder possibly have wanted?"

"Do you still feel safe working there?"

I shrugged, reluctant to admit that as soon as darkness fell I became uneasy. The image of the big, hulking shape in the doorway haunted me.

"I can send one of the male operatives to the shelter if you're uncomfortable there," he offered.

"No. I'm fine. The men are used to me. They'd be suspicious of someone new." I sighed. "It's just that I'm not getting anywhere. What if our murderer has moved on?"

Barney picked up his pipe and stared at it.

"I don't think he's moved on. It's someone local with an agenda of his own. I also think he's not finished yet."

"I just wish we had some idea why he's picking on the homeless."

"Knowing his motive would help in finding him," Barney agreed. "Tell you what. Stay at the shelter until after the holidays. If we have no results by then we'll tell Miss Sorensen that we're off the case. Agreed?"

As eager as I was to get off this hopeless case I refused to throw in the towel. "Agreed."

"There's another case you can work on in your down time. Interested?"

"Oh, yes. What is it?"

"It's a divorce case."

I did a double take. "I thought the agency didn't take divorce cases."

"We don't usually." Barney took his time lighting his pipe.

The fact that he lit it was highly unusual. Ordinarily he just fiddled with it.

"This is a special case. Personal. It involves an old army buddy from my Vietnam days."

"He's thinking about divorcing his wife?" I asked.

"No. It concerns his daughter. He thinks his son-in-law is cheating on her."

"Why doesn't she just dump him? It's relatively easy to get a divorce these days."

"Not necessarily. Not when there's a good deal of money involved. Her money. And there's a complicated prenup agreement."

"I thought those were designed to prevent a financial mess in case the marriage fell apart," I said.

"Usually they are. All depends on the stipulations and the wordings."

"So what's my assignment?"

"We're putting him under twenty-four-hour surveillance."

"And you want me to take a shift?"

"Part of one. I want you to continue part-time at the shelter, say fixing one meal, and then split one surveillance shift of the son-in-law with Glenn. That also means that he'll be near the shelter only a few hours in the evening. Are you okay with that?"

"Yes." I took my address book from my purse and glanced through it. "We'll have to find someone to cook the other meal."

"Miss Sorensen has already lined up a church group to fix breakfast. She'll be there to supervise and lend a hand."

"Great. The menus are already planned for the next two weeks. When do I start?"

"Tomorrow morning, if you can."

"I can. Where do I go?"

Barney took a manila envelope from his desk and handed it to me.

The first thing I saw was a snapshot of a woman.

"She looks familiar," I said, trying to remember where I'd seen her. "Is this the other woman?"

"No. That's our client. Her husband is our subject. She belongs to the Junior League and is on a lot of committees that help the community. You may have seen her picture in the paper."

"Yes. Her photo appears regularly on the community news page as well as on the society page. She does a lot of good for this town. And she's an attractive woman. Tell me, Uncle Barney, why does a man with a wife like this stray?"

"That's the question of the ages," he said between puffs on his pipe.

"Because he can?"

Uncle Barney lifted an eyebrow and hitched his shoulders slightly, his gesture for "it could be."

"To risk a marriage, to inflict pain so carelessly, is really, really sleazy." Just then I was hit with the intense desire to nail this creep. "You have a photo of this paragon?"

Wordlessly, he handed me a studio portrait.

I stared at it. The man was truly handsome. Not to me because I knew he was a two-timing, lying, sneaking cheat. "Women probably throw themselves at him," I said, disgusted. There wasn't much else in the envelope, except a typed sheet containing information. The man's name was Ron Dowd. His wife's name was Margot Chesterton Dowd. "Chesterton as in Chesterton Chemicals?"

"Yes, and as in Chesterton Trucking and several other businesses."

"Does this Ron work?"

"Supposedly in the chemical division of Chesterton. He has a degree in chemistry," Barney said.

"You said 'supposedly' because?"

"According to his father-in-law he doesn't put in a lot of hours at work. Claims that playing golf with prospective customers is more valuable than anything else."

I uttered a high-pitched grunt of disbelief.

Barney shrugged. "If he's incompetent it's better to put him on the golf course where he can do no damage."

"With all this snow on the ground he can't play golf. What does he do now?"

"The Sports Club has an indoor driving range."

I'd forgotten that but then I wasn't a member of that exclusive club. Nor did I play golf if I could help it. I found it a slow, boring game.

"Does Margot suspect he's cheating with a specific woman?"

"Yes. His secretary."

"Can this get any more clichéd? What time does Ron usually leave the house in the morning?"

"Rarely before nine, according to his father-in-law."

I looked at the address. "Ravenwood. Isn't that one of those gated communities in the county?"

"Yes. You'll have to pick up his tail outside the gates."

"I better drive over there early to study the neighborhood. What kind of car does he drive?"

"A vintage Corvette and a Jeep. In this weather I suspect he'll drive the Jeep. Drive carefully, Cybil. It's started to snow again."

IN THE MORNING THE SIDE roads were slick but the salt trucks had been busy on the main thoroughfares.

Ravenwood was about three miles outside the city limits, an exclusive world unto itself. A circular drive led past the gate so that those who had no business there could hightail it right back where they came from.

As I drove slowly past the gate and the guard sitting in his little house, I heard snowplows clearing the streets and driveways. No snow shoveling for the residents of Ravenwood. I felt a smidgeon of resentment, having spent an hour clearing my drive and sidewalk with a shovel.

There was no place close for me to park where the guard couldn't see me. I had no choice but to drive some fifty yards down the road where it curved sharply around a stand of trees. I parked on the shoulder, waiting for Ron Dowd's Jeep. To pass the time I looked again at the information in the packet Uncle Barney had given me. Then I examined the contents of my emergency disguise kit: Three wigs, one blond, one black, and one bright auburn, glasses, a hat, a knit cap, and makeup.

This morning I felt like being a redhead. I pinned my hair as flat to my head as I could before I slipped the wig on. The mop of short red curls gave me a vaguely Orphan Annie look. I applied an orange-based lipstick and thought I really looked quite different from my usually more subdued appearance.

I was ready for the philandering Ron Dowd.

SIX

THE SUN ROSE AND LENT the illusion of warmth to the pale, wintry morning. I kept having to run the motor at ten-minute intervals to keep from freezing as I sat in my car.

A school bus drove past and returned fifteen minutes later carrying a handful of children. I suspected that most of the offspring of the Ravenwood residents were college-age or older. After all, it took a good while to reach the income bracket that allowed the purchase of a house here. Unless you were Ron Dowd and married money. Slowly the number of cars leaving the subdivision increased as people left for work.

I hid behind an open map pretending to study it, but used the rearview mirror to watch all approaching cars. Quite a few four-wheel-drive vehicles left Ravenwood before the Jeep I'd been waiting for came into view. Nine forty-five. Ron kept banker's hours. *Must be nice,* I thought sourly, having sat shivering in my car for the last two hours.

I'd seen him clearly for only an instant, but long enough to see that he wore a beige overcoat which was undoubtedly cashmere, and a silk scarf around his neck, the kind pilots in World War Two movies wore. And he looked just as dashing as they did.

I allowed him a modest head start. He wasn't dressed for the Sports Club so I deduced he was probably headed for his office in the Chesterton Building downtown. Even he would have to show up occasionally to maintain the pretense that he worked there.

Naturally he had his own parking space in the company lot, leaving me to circle the block in search of a place to park. I finally found a metered parking space. Parallel parking had never been my strong suit, so it took three tries before I maneuvered my Volvo into position. By digging through my big shoulder bag, I located six quarters which I fed into the parking meter. Before long I'd have to get change or move the car.

The Chesterton Building was ten stories high, the third tallest downtown structure. I didn't think the various family enterprises took up all ten stories. As I reached the building entrance I saw that my guess had been correct. The first floor was taken up by the Westport Children's Clinic, one of Margot Chesterton Dowd's projects. The clinic offered free or low cost medical services for the children of Westport's poorer residents.

I took the elevator to the second floor where I found a large dental clinic and the offices of various family aid services. The elevator did not go to the next eight floors.

I went back outside where I noticed a smaller door leading to the lobby of Chesterton Enterprises. Behind a desk facing the door sat an armed guard. Unobtrusively I slipped back outside. Using my cell phone, I called Uncle Barney and reported my dilemma.

"I'll need a good cover to get inside Chesterton Enterprises," I said. "Though whether that's necessary at this point I don't know. Surely he's not brazen or dumb enough to carry on with his secretary on the premises during business hours."

"Never underestimate the stupidity of someone flaunting the rules of normal social behavior or the law. People like that never think they'll get caught."

Uncle Barney was probably right. I waited for him to come up with a suggestion.

"We'll work up a background for you by tomorrow. Today just stick around until three when Glenn will take over."

I thanked him and hung up. I went into the bank and bought a roll of quarters. From the service desk where I pretended to study a brochure on investments, I could see the entrance of the Chesterton Building. Good place to get warm. I would have liked to stay there longer but the bank guard was taking an interest in me. Time to get back to my car. Later I was glad that I had.

Kelli Morris, whom I recognized from the photo in the packet as the alleged lover, left the building dressed for outdoors. She walked to the corner and stopped, fiddling with her leather gloves. I suspected she was waiting for someone. Glancing at my watch, I discovered that it was time for an early lunch. As I debated whether to follow her on foot or risk losing my parking space, I saw Ron head for his car. Making an illegal U-turn, I came up behind him as he pulled out of the lot. At the corner he paused long enough for Kelli to hop into his car. All this was done smoothly and quickly, suggesting this was not the first time they had met like this. Intrigued, I wondered where they were going.

I stayed one car length behind the Jeep as it drove east on Buchanan. They were heading away from downtown and its many restaurants. Ron caught the yellow light on Linden and Buchanan and made a fast turn into the apartment complex on Linden. The car in front of me stopped for the red light so I had to stop as well. The light seemed to stay red forever and by the time I turned into the complex, there was no sign of the Jeep.

The complex was much larger than I had anticipated. I spent fifteen minutes looking for Ron's Jeep before I called Uncle Barney and told him that I had lost the subject. I hated doing this but had no choice. "I'm sorry, I lost him."

"It happens, Cybil. Don't beat yourself up over it."

"I know he didn't have time to turn around in the complex and head out again. I would have seen him. He just disappeared!" I felt frazzled and frustrated.

"If I remember correctly from the time I was on stakeout there a few years ago, there's a service road that connects those apartments with the ones on Randall. The Chesterton Towers," Barney said. "He could have used that road to drive to the Chesterton apartments."

"You think he'd be so brazen as to set up his secretary in an apartment belonging to his wife's family?"

"Or he could be using whatever apartment wasn't rented at the time."

That didn't strike me as being any less brazen. "What if the apartment manager walked in on them?"

"What makes you think the manager wouldn't know about it?"

I hadn't even thought of that. Slip the manager a twenty-dollar bill and why would he mention a temporary occupancy to anyone?

"What are you going to do now?" Barney asked.

"Find that Jeep." It was bad enough to lose a subject under surveillance but not to find it again was unforgivable.

Very slowly I drove through the complex looking for that service road. On my second swing I saw what in summer must have been a gravel path curving around a service shed. The only thing that marked

it as a road were fresh tire tracks. This had to be it.
I eased the Volvo through the snow, trying to stay
in the tracks made by the Jeep. I didn't want to get
stuck here.

Sure enough, the path took me to the Chesterton
apartments. Though I had driven past the apartment
complex many times I had never taken a close look
at it. The sheer size of it surprised me. Most of the
parking slots were empty, suggesting that the occupants were young enough to be out working. The
empty spaces also made it easy to spot the Jeep. I
pulled up next to it and read the sign which said that
it occupied the spot belonging to Apartment 201-D.

After I moved my car to the other side of the complex, I walked back to take a closer look at 201-D.
Less than ten minutes had elapsed since Ron Dowd
and friend had arrived at the apartment. Even for
a quick afternoon assignation this was hardly long
enough. I figured it was safe enough for me to look
around.

The vestibule of the unit served four apartments:
Two downstairs and two upstairs. The name plates
of three units listed occupants but the slot for 201-D
was empty. It didn't take a rocket scientist to figure
out that the lovers were there.

Since there was no place to hide in the small vestibule, I returned to my car. Forty minutes later, when
my feet were growing numb in my fur-lined boots,
Ron and Kelli came out and drove off.

On the way back toward downtown, Ron went through the drive-through of a fast food place. Big spender. The least he could have done was to spring for a decent lunch instead of the $3.99 special at Hamburger Haven. I hadn't thought my opinion of Ron Dowd could sink any lower but it did.

I found a parking spot half a block from the Chesterton Building downtown and started a new crossword puzzle. I didn't dare read a book as I might get so caught up in it that I'd forget to glance at the building every few minutes. With a puzzle there was no danger of that.

Half an hour later, Glenn's car drew up even with mine. I rolled my window down.

Leaning across the seat, he said, "I'm here to relieve you."

"Good. I'm starving. Our subject and his inamorata already enjoyed an afternoon…um…I don't know what the proper word is…"

"An afternoon delight?" Glenn said and grinned.

"An afternoon tryst, so it's probable that they'll go to their respective homes after work. Still, you better follow him."

"Will do. See you later at the shelter. I want your parking space." Glenn moved his car back a few feet, allowing me to pull out. We both ignored the honking horns of irate drivers behind him.

Still wondering whether the apartment they'd used was a regular love nest or merely an unrented place,

I decided to drive back to the Chesterton Towers. I'd get something to eat later.

The manager was eager to show me several apartments. He was less eager to let me into the only available upstairs apartment facing east which was the love nest, but I insisted. It was furnished and thus cost more. What he considered furnished I called partially furnished with mismatched items from a secondhand store.

In the living room a sofa, an armchair, and a coffee table huddled in the middle of the room, facing a television on a stand. The small kitchen contained the usual appliances but I doubted that anyone had cooked in it recently. A king-size bed dominated the bedroom. A bedspread had been clumsily thrown over the bedding in a poor attempt at straightening the room.

The bathroom seemed to be the most lived-in room in the place. The medicine cabinet contained both men's and women's cosmetics. The shower curtain was still damp from recent use. A hair dryer and curling iron were still plugged into an electric outlet though they had been turned off. A couple of wet towels lay on the floor.

The manager's cell phone rang. He turned away to answer it. I took the opportunity to snap a couple of photos of the toiletries in the bathroom. While he talked, I returned to the bedroom and photographed the half-made bed. Whether we'd ever need these

snapshots I had no idea. Still, it was too good an opportunity to pass up.

When he rejoined me, I said, "I thought you said
it wasn't rented." I looked pointedly at the wet towels.

The manager's face reddened. With as much dig-
nity as he could muster, he said, "This is no hot-sheet
establishment. We rent some units out on a monthly
basis."

"Who cleans up the apartments?"

"A cleaning service comes in every other week
or so."

"Who owns the apartment complex?"

"Mr. and Mrs. Dowd."

"Really? So why is it called Chesterton Towers?"

"I guess it used to be owned by Chesterton Enterprises," he said and shrugged. He walked toward
the door, a clear indication that the visit was over.

"So this apartment isn't really for rent, is it?"

"I'll have to check," he said, not looking at me.
He locked the apartment door behind us.

Outside we parted. I had the impression he wanted
to get away from me and my questions as fast as possible. I stopped on the sidewalk trying to decide what
to do next but it was too cold to linger. I slid into my
car and cranked up the heat.

I was still hungry but none of the fast food places
I passed appealed to me, and I wasn't in the mood
for a restaurant meal by myself. I drove home.

Buddy ran to meet me. I petted her, and she purred before she lapsed into growling. She gave my hand a playful bite, followed by a couple of quick licks of her pink tongue. Talk about ambiguous reactions.

"Well, what shall we have for lunch?" Always interested in food about which she had no ambiguous feelings, the kitten followed me to the kitchen and stood next to me as I looked into the fridge.

I found half an English cucumber, baby carrots, and a carton of hummus to dip them into. Plain yogurt rounded out the meal. Buddy disdained the hummus but eagerly lapped the yogurt I'd spooned into a saucer for her.

After lunch I checked my mail and paid the utility bills before I left for the shelter.

I DIDN'T SO MUCH AS CATCH A glimpse of Glenn near the shelter all evening. I didn't expect to see him while serving dinner but I thought he'd stop in the kitchen afterward for his usual cup of coffee. Had something happened to him? I waited ten more anxious minutes before I phoned Uncle Barney.

"It's probably nothing but Glenn hasn't checked in with me tonight. He always does as soon as the dining room is cleaned up. Have you heard from him?"

"No. I'll be right over."

As always, Uncle Barney didn't ask unnecessary questions or waste words. Since he was at home it took him a little longer to get to the shelter. I spent the time assembling the dry ingredients for next morning's pancakes.

He had dressed appropriately for the neighborhood. Instead of the three-piece suits he wore to the office, he'd chosen corduroy pants, a sweatshirt, a heavy peacoat, and a wool cap.

"I know this area so I'm going with you," I said before he had a chance to object. I grabbed my parka and gloves.

We circled the block closest to the shelter before we walked farther away.

"This is odd," I said when we didn't see a single homeless person near the church. "Where is everybody?"

"You suppose the cops made one of their periodic sweeps through the neighborhood and rounded up as many of the homeless as they could and scared the others into hiding?" he asked.

"I didn't hear any sirens. The cops usually arrive with lights flashing and sirens screaming."

"But something did scare them away. If not the cops, then who or what?" Barney wondered out loud.

"Look! There's Pete. Maybe he knows." I waved to Pete, who'd emerged from the alley, and motioned to him to join us.

I made the introductions before I asked, "Pete, where is everyone?"

"There was a big fight. Knives. It got pretty serious. One guy tried to break it up and he got hurt. Everyone ran off."

I had a very bad feeling about this. "The guy who got hurt. Do you know him?"

"No. He's new."

Uncle Barney and I looked at each other thinking the same awful thing.

"Any idea where we can find him?" Barney asked.

"My guess is that he's hiding in one of the abandoned buildings until he feels it's safe enough to come out and get help."

"Okay, let's go back to the shelter and start the search from there," I suggested.

"I'll take the west side of the street," Pete offered.

Back at the shelter we parted.

Uncle Barney and I started at a fast pace through the alley. I almost missed the dark spots in the snow.

"Uncle Barney, shine your flashlight over here." The urgency in my voice stopped him from asking anything. He shone the powerful beam of his light on the drops in the snow. We both squatted down for a closer look.

"Blood?" I asked, my voice faint. The sight of blood always made me feel queasy.

"Wait here," he said and followed the red drops in the snow.

No way was I staying behind. I hurried after him, careful to step in his footsteps. No sense in messing up a crime scene if that's what this was. The blood drops led us to the shed behind the parsonage of the Church of Holiness.

"The door's been opened since the new snowfall this afternoon," Barney whispered, pointing his light beam on the markings in the snow.

My eyes widened when I saw him draw his Glock from the holster under his coat. He didn't often carry his gun and that he did now made me even more afraid for Glenn.

"Stay here," he whispered.

I nodded and watched him yank the door open and, crouching down, sprint inside. I picked up a small branch that the wind had torn from a tree and tested it in my hand as a possible weapon. It wasn't much of one but it was better than nothing.

"Cybil, in here."

I dropped the branch and dashed into the shed.

"Over here."

Uncle Barney was bent over a figure, half lying, half sitting in the corner. It was too dark to see clearly but there was something familiar about the man.

"Glenn? Is that you?"

"Yeah." He groaned when he tried to get up.

He was obviously hurt. "How bad is it?"

Barney handed me his cell phone. "Call an ambulance."

"No! That'll blow my cover. No ambulance," Glenn insisted. "It's just a knife cut."

"Dial Luke's number, please. Maybe he can come."

I stepped outside to make the call. Luke said he'd come as quickly as he could. Seeing me, Pete ran across the yard.

"You found the man who got hurt?" he asked.

"Yes."

"How is he?"

"A doctor is on the way. Come on inside."

Pete followed me into the shed. "Luke's coming," I announced. "He said not to move Glenn until he got here. How bad is the bleeding?"

"It's slowed down. I packed snow into my knit hat and pressed it against the wound. I think the cold slowed the bleeding."

I didn't know if this was an old wives' tale or if the cold actually did slow down the bleeding. You'd think having been married to a physician all those years some medical knowledge would have rubbed off on me but it hadn't. When we talked about medicine, it was mostly from a social worker's point of view: Why we didn't have a national health-care plan, where patients could get inexpensive medications, what free immunizations were available for infants, stuff like that.

"Pete and I will wait outside. I'm not sure Luke knows exactly where we are," I said.

We walked down to the street. Then an alarming

thought hit me. "Pete, what are the chances that the guy who cut Glenn might be back?"

He shrugged. "It's not likely. He's got half a bottle of schnapps and a place to crash."

I saw Luke park his car and ran to meet him. "Thanks for coming. Glenn's in the shed back there." Pete joined us on the way, and I introduced him to Luke. Pete offered to stand guard outside the shed.

The first thing Luke said was that he needed more light. "Cybil, hold my flashlight."

His was also a big utility light, which I focused on Glenn's body. Luke made a quick examination.

"You really should come to the emergency room. You'll need stitches. When was the last time you had a tetanus shot?"

"I don't remember, but it's been a while," Glenn said.

From his voice I could tell that he was in considerable pain now that the adrenaline from the fight had worn off.

"Why don't we go into the shelter?" I said to Glenn.

Supported by Luke on one side and Uncle Barney on the other, Glenn's feet barely touched the ground as we rushed to the shelter. Pete carried Luke's medical bag. I ran ahead and unlocked the back door. I didn't turn on any lights until I'd drawn the curtains.

"This pine table gets a good scrubbing every evening," I said. "I'll get a sheet. We always bleach our sheets, so they're really clean. Luke, you can wash up back there," I said, pointing to the staff bathroom.

By the time I returned with the sheet, they'd removed Glenn's coat, jacket and shirt. When I saw the bloody slash across Glenn's ribs I gasped. Luke took one look at me and sent me off to make tea.

"Make it strong and sweet. Barney will assist me here. And Pete, if he's not squeamish."

"I'm not. I'll be glad to do whatever is necessary."

Meekly I went and put on the kettle. I don't know why I was such a wuss—totally useless in a medical situation. I busied myself with setting out cups and raiding the emergency stash of cookies. After tonight's events we could all use a fast boost of energy.

I walked to the back door and opened it to get a quick breath of cold, fresh air. That's when I saw that big, bulky figure again hurriedly disappearing down the alley. I quickly closed the door and locked it. Who was that man? And why was he hanging around the shelter?

SEVEN

WE GATHERED AT THE SHELTER'S kitchen counter for tea and *Spitzbuben,* jam-filled shortbread cookies Maxi had baked.

Glenn looked a little pale but that didn't keep him from devouring a handful of cookies.

"What was the fight about?" I asked.

Glenn shrugged. "A couple of the guys were passing a bottle of peppermint schnapps around. Earl claimed that Howie took two swigs instead of one and one thing led to another."

"They pulled knives on each other over some vile alcohol that probably tastes worse than mouthwash?" But even as I asked I knew I shouldn't have. I sounded like such a Pollyanna.

"On a cold winter's night a swig to warm you up is nothing to sneeze at," Glenn said. "And it is cold out there tonight." He shivered, remembering the icy wind.

"You're going home now and getting some rest," Barney said. He turned to Luke. "Glenn should stay in bed tomorrow as well?"

"Yes. Come to my office in the ER around one and

ask for me. I'll check the wound for infection. Not that I expect any problems, but I want to be sure."

"I'll drive you home," Barney said. "Someone from the agency will get your car."

"And I'll walk Cybil to her car," Luke offered, picking up his medical bag. "You have a place to stay?" Luke asked Pete.

"Yeah, in the dormitory. Thanks for asking."

We all walked out together and said good night.

THE NEXT MORNING UNCLE Barney handed me a folder containing my new identity, which had landed me a job as a temp at Chesterton Enterprises. According to my dossier I was a good typist and adept at word processing. That was true enough. As to the shorthand skills the dossier mentioned I was on shaky ground. I hadn't used my shorthand skills since my counseling days when I took notes during sessions with a client. Since Mrs. Chesterton Dowd had hired me to investigate her hubby, I doubted that she'd call me in for dictation.

Dressed in a navy skirt, a crisp white blouse with a silk navy-and-red scarf tied around my neck, and wearing a pair of granny glasses with clear glass in them, I reported for duty at eight. The office manager, a middle-aged woman with a harried expression, led me to a cubicle and handed me several pages of notes which I was to put into report form and type on a word processor.

The computer program the company used was the one that presumed to correct my grammar and punctuation, which irritated me no end. As far as I knew, the rules of punctuation and grammar hadn't been changed yet. I muttered unkind things about the computer's ancestry when the wavy lines underlined parts of my composition which I knew were correct in traditional grammar. On top of that, my glasses pinched the bridge of my nose and I regretted wearing them. The harried office manager would hardly notice if I took them off, so I did and felt better.

At noon I went to the employees' cafeteria where I bought a sandwich and a pot of tea. As I was a little late, having lost my way in the endless corridors, all the tables were taken. I paused, tray in hand, undecided where to go.

"This chair isn't taken," a voice to my left announced.

I turned in the direction of the voice which belonged to a woman who wasn't far from retirement. "Thank you, Debbie." I put my tray on the table for two and sat down.

"How'd you know my name?"

"Your name tag."

"Oh, yeah." She smiled a little self-consciously. "What department are you working in?"

"I'm a temp. I go wherever help is needed."

"We sure could use you in our section. But we hardly ever get any extra help." She sighed.

"And why is that?" She shrugged and looked at me, clearly deciding if she ought to say anything else. Apparently I looked trustworthy enough.

Leaning toward me, Debbie said in a low voice, "I might as well tell you because you'll hear about it anyway. It's because of Kelli."

I took a sip of tea and waited. After a beat she continued.

"We all suspect she's fooling around with the boss's husband."

"Oh. I thought Mr. Dowd was the boss."

"Well, he is. Sort of. But Mrs. Dowd's maiden name is Chesterton. She practically owns the whole company."

"Does everyone suspect that Kelli is fooling around?"

"Everyone on our floor, except Mrs. Dowd." Debbie paused. "Though I'm wondering if she's not just ignoring the affair. They never last long."

"So this isn't his first fling with an employee?"

"I was here before Mrs. Dowd married him. They were hardly back from the honeymoon when his eyes started to roam. He's an awful flirt. I don't know why she doesn't just kick him out."

I had wondered the same thing until I learned about the prenup. "Maybe it would be bad for the business."

Debbie snorted. "I can't see how. He doesn't do a

whole lot. It's Mr. Chesterton and Mrs. Dowd who do the work. And us."

"So he's just…decorative?"

"That sums it up. He *is* good-looking, if you like the pretty-boy type."

I didn't, and Debbie obviously didn't either. I took a bite of my sandwich and chewed and chewed and chewed before I could swallow. Separating the two pieces of bread, I studied the filling.

Debbie giggled. "Dry as cardboard?"

I nodded with a grimace.

"You're better off bringing your lunch. I always do. Better and cheaper. You can keep it in the fridge over there."

Right about now one of my peanut butter-banana-honey sandwiches sounded mighty good. I pulled the lonely slice of cheese from the middle and ate it, ignoring the stale, white slices of bread.

The afternoon passed slowly. The stuff I was typing had to do with chemicals and I understood it about as well as I did ancient Greek.

On my afternoon break I observed Ron Dowd in action. Getting a cup of coffee, which I suspected was a mere pretext to be in the employee lounge, he stopped at tables where young, pretty employees sat. The rest of us he ignored.

When Kelli came into the room Ron left quickly, but I was fairly sure she had seen him flirt with the lovely redhead who probably graduated from high school this past June. Kelli did not look happy.

Ron left work early and so did I. While he used the driving range at the Sports Club I sat in my car. I was tired of crossword puzzles so I picked up my knitting. However, my fingers were too cold and stiff so I gave up and merely stared through the windshield. I sighed in frustration. Sitting and waiting was the worst part of being an investigator.

Two hours later I followed him to his subdivision and then drove home.

The following day was a repeat of the first except instead of meeting Kelli for an early afternoon delight he met the redhead after work. The man was a moral sleaze. I suspected the only reason he didn't take the redhead to Chesterton Towers was that some of Kelli's things were there. Instead, he took his new love interest to a cheap motel.

Since the manager of this establishment spent his time fingering his sparse, ginger-colored mustache and staring out the window, I couldn't park in front of one of the empty units but circled a three-block area around the motel. I had managed to zoom in and snap a photo of the redhead and Ron entering the same motel room. The room number was visible in each photo with the date and time on the bottom. I also took a long shot of the Clearview Motel, though what they had a view of, clear or otherwise, I couldn't tell.

Ron, ever the romantic lover, was the first to leave, but instead of heading toward home or back to the office, he took the highway south out of town. Surely he wasn't planning to drive all the way to Indianapolis? By now I was so hungry that the two slices of white bread I'd disdained the day before appeared downright appetizing.

Fortunately, his turn signal indicated that he was pulling into what I assume was a strip mall. Just before turning and following him, I realized this was Classic Greens and Garden Services and wrenched my car back onto the road. I would have had a hard time explaining my presence to Frederick Holmes at his establishment after closing hours. Come to think of it, what was Ron doing here?

I pulled into the strip mall across the street, turned my car so it pointed toward the highway and parked. Three of the four businesses in this mall were closed for the day but the fourth, a pizza place, was open. The seductive aroma wafting from its exhaust system made me even hungrier. If this surveillance went on much longer I'd have to start keeping snacks in the car. While Ron sat in his Jeep I almost dashed into the pizza parlor to buy a couple of slices.

Good thing that I didn't because Ron got out of his Jeep when a tall man came from the back of the garden store. Though I didn't think he could see me with the highway between us and the fading daylight, I slid down in my seat a little when I recognized

Frederick Holmes. The men stood a few feet apart and talked. The conversation started out apparently civilized enough, but judging by the body language and the gestures used it didn't remain so. For a moment I thought the encounter might turn physical but then Frederick took an envelope from his coat pocket and threw it at the younger man, who caught it deftly.

Ron jumped into his Jeep and took off toward town, narrowly missing a collision with a south-bound van. More cautiously I pulled onto the highway and followed him to his gated subdivision.

I phoned Uncle Barney and reported what I'd seen.

"What kind of envelope was it?" he wanted to know.

"A regular white business envelope."

"Did Ron check what was in it?"

"He opened the flap and appeared to be satisfied with what he saw." I thought for a moment. "What sort of business brings a nursery owner and a chemist together?"

"Don't forget that Frederick Holmes also owns a fertilizer plant. He employs chemists. Maybe Ron is a consultant."

This still seemed thin to me but I didn't say so. "What do you want me to do now?"

"Come on in. Mrs. Dowd will be at the agency at six-thirty." Drat. Not enough time to get a slice of pizza.

TWO HOURS LATER I SET the table in my kitchen while my grandmother reheated the food she had brought.

"Good thing I fixed stew. It tastes even better reheated," Maxi said.

It was typical of Maxi not to scold me for being late for dinner. I knew she was watching me so I tried hard to be upbeat, but I couldn't fool her.

"What's wrong, Schatzi?" she asked after serving the food.

"This case. I've been following this…man who's cheating on his wife. Not with just one woman, but with two—two that I know of. I hope she divorces his sorry butt."

"Do you think she will?"

"I don't know. Her face was like a mask when she looked at the photos I took of him and his girlfriends. I couldn't look her in the eye, I felt so rotten for her."

"I'm surprised Barney took this case."

"Only as a special favor to a friend." Then an alarming thought hit me. "What if—" I shook my head.

"What, Schatzi?"

"What if she does something really drastic?"

"Like shooting or poisoning her miserable, cheating hubby?"

I nodded.

"I hope not. He doesn't sound like he's worth serious penitentiary time."

"Believe me, he isn't. But she must feel rejected? Betrayed? Unloved?"

Maxi nodded. "I'm sure she's feeling all those emotions but I hope anger will be at the top of the list. Cold fury when she contacts an attorney. She deserves to get every penny of his money."

I merely hoped it wasn't going to be the other way around.

"Any news on the murders at the shelter?" Maxi asked.

"No. Everything's been quiet. If we could only come up with a motive."

"Maybe the murderer left town," Maxi said.

"I hope not." That didn't sound right. "What I mean is that I want to catch whoever poisoned Duchess." I spooned a little more gravy from the stew onto Buddy's saucer and added a couple of small pieces of meat. She seemed to appreciate Maxi's stew as much as I did. She even ate a tiny piece of carrot.

On Saturday morning my car wouldn't start. My fault for not putting it into the garage but I'd had no idea that the temperature would drop into the single digits. I needed to watch the weather reports, I reminded myself.

I jogged to the agency to use one of the cars we kept there. The only one in that morning was the four-door sedan, a considerably bigger car than I was used to driving. I felt like I was in a tank, but on snowy roads the extra weight was actually a benefit.

Parking outside the subdivision's gate and out of sight of the guard's hut, I poured myself a cup of black coffee from my thermos. It was a new blend called Earth, Wind, and Fire. I liked it a lot and sipped it slowly.

This being a Saturday, there was no telling how late Ron would sleep in. Lucky him. I resigned myself to a long wait. I yawned and drank some more coffee.

To my surprise, the Jeep left the subdivision at 9:30. As per standard agency procedure, I let him get a head start. I was about to pull into the street when a car shot through the gate and accelerated furiously. A silver Avanti. The only person I knew who drove such a car was Margot Chesterton Dowd. Where was she going in such a rush?

I followed, driving faster than I liked to drive on snow-covered roads. Fortunately, she slowed down a few minutes later. When I rounded the curve I saw why. She had her husband's Jeep in sight. I expected her to close the gap between them but she didn't. She kept far enough back not to call attention to herself but close enough to... Then it hit me. Margot was following her husband. Why? She had told us to stay on the job and we were. Did she no longer trust us? Had something happened between them?

A few minutes later I realized Ron was headed to-

ward the Sports Club. Maybe they exercised together.
I relaxed, knowing now where they were going. On
the downside it would mean sitting in the car for
several hours again. I sighed and dropped back farther. Sure enough, Ron stopped to flash his ID at the
gatekeeper, who raised the guardrail with a jaunty
salute. I almost slowed down to a stop, fully expect-
ing Margot to drive into the club as well. She didn't
but kept on going.

When she parked in the same spot I had when I'd
followed her husband previously, I knew my mouth
dropped open. What was she up to, and what was I
to do now? There was nothing I could do but keep
on driving.

There was no room to turn around on the narrow
road, not until I came to the four-way stop on the
county road. I made an illegal U-turn and sped back
toward the club. Margot's car was gone and I had
no idea where. Nor did I know whether Ron had left
the club while I searched for a place to turn around.
Uncle Barney would not be pleased if he knew that
I'd messed up my primary surveillance.

I had to get into the club. Once before I'd sneaked
in with relative ease but it didn't look as if it was
going to be as easy this time. Somehow I'd have to
get the guard to leave his post long enough to dash
through the gate.

Unless I was out in the country, I didn't lug bin-
oculars around with me. However, my expensive,

German-made opera glasses, a gift from Maxi, were small enough to carry in my shoulder bag and powerful enough for me to read the guard's name tag pinned to his uniform.

Next I dialed the club's switchboard and asked to speak to Burt. The operator put me through to the guard without asking any questions.

"Main gate," he said.

"Burt, this is the office. One of our guests is having car trouble. She's an important woman so please go and help her. It's the silver Avanti."

"I'm not supposed to leave—"

"Don't you think I know that? But she's upset and, as I said, influential. Go and help her now. That's an order."

I thought I heard a mumbled word that sounded suspiciously like *witch* but I wasn't sure. Besides, he was right. I'd sounded like a world-class witch.

Dutifully, Burt left his post and turned left toward the parking area. I sprinted through the gate and hunkered down beside the guard's hut. Peering around its far corner, I saw him walking to the end of the lot. I ducked into the first unlocked door and found myself in the club's laundry room. Fortunately, nobody was there.

I took one of the smocks from its hook and put it on over my parka. Then I picked up a stack of clean towels and ventured outside. If anyone challenged me, I could claim to be the maid the service agency had sent to help out. Nobody challenged me.

Undecided where to go, I paused and looked around. Where was the inside driving range?

"Hey, you!"

I turned, startled. Peering around the towels, I faced a man whose face was red and angry. He wore a maroon blazer with a gold emblem on the chest pocket. He had to be some sort of employee of the club.

"They needed the towels in the locker room ten minutes ago," he said, his voice accusing, his eyes mean.

I nodded and looked around at the buildings.

"Over there," he said and pointed. "And hurry up!"

Why people thought that they could be understood better at high decibel levels I'll never know.

"Get a move on, you—" He broke off, exasperated. Then muttering, he added, "Why we can't get decent help, I don't know. Ignorant trash."

"Yes, sir," I said, ignoring his reference to being ignorant trash. Since I couldn't risk his finding out that I was neither employed by the club nor a guest, I clamped my teeth together to keep silent. Feeling his eyes on my back, I had no choice but to enter the building he had pointed to.

The stack of towels in my arms was tall enough to obstruct my vision. Peeking around the towels I saw a door marked LOCKER ROOM. I managed to open it without dropping the towels and walked in.

"Woman coming in," an amused male voice called out. A wolf whistle and whooping sounds followed. As if propelled by a jolt of electricity I bolted out of the room and jerked the door shut behind me. Across the hall was another door marked LOCKER ROOM. I dashed inside and paused to catch my breath.

The room seemed to be empty. I stood, rooted to the spot, until my heart rate slowed down. Instead of the strong odor of old sweat that had hit me as soon as I opened the men's locker room, here the air was filled with a floral air freshener, the scent of shampoo, soap and perfume. Patchouli and roses? I looked at my watch and made myself wait five minutes before I opened the door an inch and looked across the hall. Sure enough the door sported the figure of a man above the locker room sign. The towels had prevented me from seeing it.

Glancing around the ladies' locker room, I noticed that they had a big stack of clean towels already. The ones I carried were meant for the men. I stood, undecided. Maybe I could just leave them outside the door? No. If someone needed a towel they'd want it when they stepped out of the shower. On the other hand I had to give those men enough time to get dressed. I sat down and waited ten minutes. Then my patience ran out.

"Oh, for heaven's sake. Open the door and toss

them in," I told myself. Still I hesitated, not wanting to encounter more men in their natural glory. On the other hand, I couldn't remain in the women's locker room all day either. Sooner or later someone was bound to come in. I took a breath and crossed the hall.

Forcefully I knocked on the men's door but there was no reply. I knocked again, then opened the door and dropped the towels on the white, plastic chair beside it. I quickly pulled the door shut and froze.

The foot. Why had I seen a bare foot on the other side of the long bench in front of the lockers? Not a bare foot standing but lying on the cold tile floor? And not just a foot. I was pretty sure there was a leg attached to it. A long, hairy leg.

Every impulse in my body urged me to run, but my conscience commanded that I take a second look. Maybe someone had slipped on the wet tiles and needed help?

I opened the door a crack. "Hello?" My voice was weak but audible. "Hello?" I repeated more loudly and opened the door wider. As I did, I saw the body sprawled on the far side of the bench. It wore beige trunks. Something wet and red had pooled around it. The liquid seemed to have leaked…maybe was still leaking…from the chest, from that object that stuck out of it. The handle of a knife, the kind of knife we used at the shelter to slice things, thin-bladed and sharp. I saw all this in the instant before I let out a sound that was halfway between a gasp and a muted scream.

Think, Cybil.

I forced myself to walk to the body. Bending down, I moved my fingers up and down his throat but couldn't find a pulse. It was only then that I looked at the face and flinched. I knew that face, that person. I'd been assigned to follow him but I hadn't followed him closely enough and now he was dead.

I sank to my knees and stared helplessly, hopelessly.

Then I heard a stealthy sound, like someone moving carefully, slowly, to avoid making a noise. My body froze, wondering if a knife was inches from being plunged into my back. No! I wasn't going to wait to become another victim. With a cry I hoped sounded ferocious, I jumped up and turned, ready to lunge at whoever was behind me, but all I saw was the emergency door to the outside closing fast.

Why wasn't the alarm going off, I wondered as I sprinted toward the door. I dashed up the three stairs to the sidewalk. I ran to the end of the building, turned, slipped on a patch of ice. I hit the ground hard. Embarrassed I got up quickly, brushed the snow off my clothes, and looked around. I didn't think anyone had witnessed my less-than-graceful encounter with the sidewalk.

The scene before me looked totally normal. A group of four women, talking animatedly with exercise bags slung over their shoulders, walked toward the entrance. Two men left the building where the racquetball courts were located, carrying their racquets and probably discussing their game. The woman who led the aerobics class at the YWCA was hurrying toward the building. She probably taught a class here as well. I saw no one running away in a panic. And yet he was somewhere in this area.

As I stood there, undecided what to do, I heard a commotion in the building behind me. Someone else had found the body. I heaved a sigh of relief. Now I would not have to be the one phoning the police and explaining to them, and worse, explaining to my cousin, Lieutenant Sam Keller, what I'd been doing in the men's locker room of this exclusive club. For once I might escape Sam's interrogation. This stroke of luck made me think of Maxi's saying about even a blind hen sometimes finding a kernel of grain.

Word of something happening seemed to spread fast as more people rushed toward the building. I put the hood of my toggle coat over my head, hoping to make me less easily identifiable, and walked as quickly as I could without seeming to flee the scene. I walked along the parking area but saw no silver Avanti. Good. Hopefully, Margot Chesterton Dowd was getting her hair done or had some other ironclad alibi. I'd hate to have to implicate her in her husband's murder. As everyone knew, the nearest and dearest of the victim were always suspects.

I had hoped the guard would follow the curious members but he didn't leave his post. Just my bad luck that he was a conscientious employee. Somehow I'd have to get over the wall. When the guard turned to check a car waiting to be admitted, I ducked around the corner. The path, snow-covered, led me to the back of the building. There were several sets of footprints in the snow, but they overlapped, making them useless for identification. At least I was pretty sure they'd be useless.

When I saw a couple of service trucks, I called myself several kinds of a fool. The service entrance. Why hadn't I remembered it? I walked several steps in the tire tracks before I stopped abruptly. There was only one set of fresh tire tracks leading to the back entrance. The murderer's? Quickly I stepped out of them. The tire prints in the snow could be evidence which I could not contaminate. Yet if I walked in the fresh snow, I'd leave footprints which would misdirect the police. What should I do? I reached for my cell phone. Time to consult Uncle Barney.

EIGHT

AFTER I REPORTED TO Uncle Barney everything that had happened, he told me to stay at the club and wait for the police. I started to object until he told me that I had no choice but to talk to the officers. He also told me that he would be at the club as soon as possible, which made me feel a little better. I retraced my steps to the vicinity of the men's locker room.

Waiting to face the police was the last thing I wanted to do. Maybe this was Sam's day off, maybe it would be only Sergeant Griffin who came, maybe... no. Westport's PD was small, so even if it were Sam's day off he'd be called in. I resigned myself to spending most of the morning waiting to be questioned.

I took off the smock I'd borrowed and returned it to the laundry room. I didn't want to add theft to my other misdeeds. No sooner had I returned to the locker room building when I heard the police sirens. I leaned against the wall near the ladies' locker room, trying to look nonchalant.

Sam entered the building accompanied by Sergeant Griffin, who was trailed by the man wearing the club's maroon blazer, and a guy in sweats who was talking a mile a minute. He had to be the one who found the body.

When Sam saw me, he detached himself from the group and approached me with a frown on his face.

"Cybil, don't tell me you're involved in this case."

"Sort of," I mumbled guiltily.

Sam looked at the ceiling with that *why me?* expression I knew so well. "Don't leave until I've talked to you," he said, shaking his index finger at me for emphasis. "Don't move from this spot."

"I won't," I promised, though I was dying to sit down. Or better yet, crawl into my bed and not come out for a week. Shifting from foot to foot I adjusted my position. My left side, which had borne the brunt of my earlier fall on the ice, was beginning to hurt seriously. Or maybe I was just now beginning to become aware of the pain.

The outside door opened and Uncle Barney came in. I wanted to run to him and throw my arms around him in gratitude but that would have been unprofessional, so I merely attempted to smile at him when he came to stand beside me.

"You okay?" he asked.

I nodded and then decided not to pretend. I shrugged. "I'm not sure. There was so much blood," I whispered. Uncle Barney placed his arm around my shoulders.

"Where's Sam?" he asked.

"In there," I said, pointing to the men's locker room. "With the body."

We stood in the hallway for what seemed like forever. Finally two men carrying a stretcher came out and placed the body into the ambulance. They were followed by Sam and his team. Sergeant Griffin placed yellow crime scene tape over the door.

Sam approached us. "The manager is letting us use the small dining room for our interviews. It's in the building next door. I want to talk to Cybil first."

Silently we followed him to the designated room. I took off my coat and placed it on an empty chair.

Sam motioned me to sit down.

"Cybil, why were you at the scene of the murder?"

So much for beating around the bush. I looked at Uncle Barney.

Sam frowned. "What? Why are you looking at Uncle Barney? To consult him?"

"Cybil was on a case."

"So?"

"You know our cases are confidential."

"Not in the same way a doctor's or a lawyer's are. Besides, this is a murder investigation."

I said nothing, but watched Uncle Barney fiddling with his pipe.

"Tell me what you were doing here at the club. Keep in mind that lots of people saw you."

I wasn't sure about the *lots* but some had seen

me. I glanced at Uncle Barney who nodded encouragingly.

"I followed someone here."

"Who?"

I refrained from pointing out to Sam that he should have said *whom*. "The victim. Ron Dowd."

"Aha."

Although Sam's tone implied that he expected me to confide in him I didn't elaborate.

"Well?" he snapped. "Why were you following Ron Dowd?"

"It was my assignment."

"Yeah? How long did you follow him?"

Remembering Uncle Barney's instructions never to volunteer information or embellish and elaborate, I simply said, "Several days."

"And in those several days what did he do?"

"I don't see the relevance of that for your case," Barney said.

"Maybe it's relevant and maybe it's not. Let's start with today. Where did you start to tail him?"

Uncle Barney nodded slightly. "From outside his subdivision."

"And where did you follow him to?"

"This club."

"Then what? Cybil, don't make me drag every little detail out of you," Sam warned.

"I drove to the four-way stop in the county road

to turn around and then I parked a little ways from the club."

"And?"

"Then I waited until the guard left his post and ran into the laundry room."

Sam frowned. "Why the laundry room?"

"It was the closest place that I thought would be empty."

"And was it?"

"Yes."

"Go on."

"I picked up a stack of towels and entered the men's dressing room." I told him what happened then. I concluded with, "I dropped the towels on a chair. That's when I saw the body. Someone left by the emergency exit, and I followed."

"The alarm didn't go off?" Barney asked.

"No. I wondered about that."

"We'll check it out," Sam said. "Did you see who left the room?"

"No. I didn't even catch a glimpse of him."

"And you didn't come back into the locker room?"

"No. I didn't want to see all that blood again." I shivered, knowing that the image of Ron's body was going to stay in my mind for a long time. "I looked around outside but saw no one running. Then I phoned Uncle Barney and waited in the hall. You saw me there."

"You said you followed the victim. Where did he

go to?" When Sam saw me hesitate, he added, "If it has nothing to do with this case, I'll never mention what you tell me. Are you sure it has no bearing on his murder?"

I wasn't sure. I had no idea who killed him. Could one of his lovers have done it? I couldn't picture either one of them doing it, but then I couldn't picture anyone plunging a knife into another human being's chest.

"Cybil?" Sam prompted, and Uncle Barney nodded.

"He went to work and he met two different young women from his office for an assignation."

"Now we're getting somewhere," Sam said with satisfaction.

"If you think either of those women could have done this you're way off the mark," I said, my voice full of conviction.

"Why? Because a woman couldn't stab a man? Granted, a knife usually isn't the first choice of weapon for a woman but it has happened. I'll need their names."

I told him. "They both work for Chesterton Enterprises."

"How original," Sam said sarcastically. "And convenient. The boss fooling around with two of his employees. Did they agree to the affairs voluntarily or did he apply pressure? You know what I mean. No hanky-panky, no raise, or even no job?"

"He's…he was a good-looking man. I doubt that he had to force either of them."

"There is a Mrs. Dowd, isn't there?"

I nodded.

"Wonder how she felt about hubby messing around with the hired help?"

With a start I remembered the silver Avanti parked near the back entrance of the club. I didn't dare risk a glance at Uncle Barney so I stared at the floor.

"Cybil?" Sam prompted.

"I've barely met his wife, so how could I know—"

"Why don't you ask Mrs. Dowd how she felt?" Barney suggested. "Anything we say would be nothing more than guesses and conjectures."

Thank you, Uncle Barney.

"You can bet your bottom dollar I'll ask her," Sam said. "Cybil, is there anything pertinent to this case you've forgotten to tell me?"

"I can't think of anything." That was almost the truth. The only thing I hadn't mentioned was Margot Chesterton Dowd being near the club. I'd have to talk to Uncle Barney about that omission.

Now not only the left side of my body hurt but my head ached as well. I needed about four ibuprofen pills and a place to lie down.

"If that's all," Barney said, "We'll be off."

Sam dismissed us. Only too glad to get away, we hurried outside.

"Uncle Barney, do you mind if I go home and lie

down for a while? I don't feel all that great. My head hurts fiendishly."

"I was about to suggest that you do just that. Want me to phone Luke to bring you something for your headache?"

"No, thanks. I'll be fine." I did not need my estranged husband to fuss over me and tell me how unsuited I was to my present line of work.

"Is there anything you can remember that you forgot to tell Sam?"

This was Uncle Barney's way of asking if I held anything back from my cop cousin. "I told you Margot followed Ron and parked outside the club. When I turned around at the four-way stop her car was gone. I made that call to the guard to look for the silver Avanti. I don't think he saw it. I certainly didn't when I looked for it a little while later. So she didn't go into the club and couldn't have stabbed Ron. Besides, Sam will question her anyway. And the guard." I shrugged. "But…"

"What?"

"Something keeps nagging at me, but every time I'm about to remember it's gone like a wisp of smoke."

"Don't try so hard. It'll come to you. Probably in the middle of the night."

We parted. I drove home where I fed Buddy, my ever hungry orange tabby, took four ibuprofen and lay down on the couch. Pulling my soft chenille throw over me I sighed and closed my eyes.

WHEN I WOKE UP IT WAS late afternoon. I tried to get up but fell back with a groan. My body felt stiff and sore. I should have soaked in a hot tub before I lay down. Time to remedy that.

I filled my deep, old-fashioned tub with water so hot it made me shiver when I slid in. I stayed until I looked like a boiled lobster. After consulting the weather channel and noting that the temperature had fallen, I dressed in double layers of clothes and drove to the shelter.

Maxi was already there. I hugged her super hard.

"What happened?" she asked.

"What makes you think something happened?"

"Because you hugged me with desperation." She stepped back and looked at me. "I can feel and see the aura of anxiety hovering all around you."

"Are you sure you're not psychic?"

"Just observant."

She poured us each a cup of fragrant Darjeeling tea and motioned for me to sit at the counter beside her. I did. And I told her about finding Ron.

"My poor Schatzi. You do have a talent for finding dead bodies."

I shot her a long-suffering look. "Why couldn't I have been blessed with a talent for painting, or singing, or even needlework, or anything a little less upsetting than dead bodies?"

"I don't know, dear. At least your talent is unique."

The twinkle in her intelligent blue eyes was both affectionate and amused.

"You know, people who see a silver lining in everything can be quite annoying," I told her.

"I know," she said, her voice contrite. "Drink your tea. Our hungry clients are about to descend on us."

And they did before I had a chance to finish my tea.

By the time we had served about eighty people, Maxi looked exhausted. "Tell you what. Since you cooked, I'll supervise the cleanup and you go home. You look tired. As you should, after fixing all this food."

"Are you sure…"

"I'm sure. I have help lined up." I took the dishtowel from her hand. "Doesn't your dog need to go out about now for his evening routine?"

Thinking of Hiram, she smiled. "Yes he does. He's the sweetest, cutest little thing. And such good company. I'm so grateful to you for giving him to me."

Hiram had belonged to a murder victim and rather than letting Sam take him to the pound, I'd driven him to Maxi's farm. The two had taken to each other like long-lost friends.

I said good night to Maxi and turned to the formidable task of washing the pots and pans. Pete came to help me.

"Anything new around here?" I asked in a low voice.

"No. Earl's in jail. Got into a fight and when the cops tried to break it up he resisted and they hauled him in. So it's been quiet around here."

"Maybe we were wrong. Maybe the three murders are unrelated."

"Maybe."

Pete sounded as unconvinced of that as I was. "But why would the murderer suddenly stop? And if it was only to get these three people, what did they have in common?"

"Only that they were homeless and came to this shelter."

Letting the water out of the sink I looked around. "What could it be at this shelter that someone would commit three murders for?" I shook my head. "Granted there are two buyers interested in acquiring the place, but I can't see either of them starting a murder epidemic to get it."

Pete looked doubtful.

"What?"

"Maybe greed for the place makes a little more sense than a deranged killer who hates the homeless."

"Neither makes any sense but then since when does murder make sense?"

"I need to get to the dormitory, or I'll lose my bed. Will you be okay here?"

"Yes. I'll be leaving soon. Glenn or Uncle Barney will be here, so you go on. Good night."

Alone, I wiped down the counter and since I had some time, I looked at our supplies, never having finished the original inventory. I felt a frisson of fear, a sense of déjà vu, when I found myself alone in the windowless supply room. I shook off the feeling and started to count the cans of vegetables we had. We definitely need to buy more to see us through December.

When I heard a noise that seemed to come from the back door, I froze. Not again.

Where was Uncle Barney? Glenn? I turned off the pantry's light. Ducking down to make myself a smaller target, I scooted into the dark kitchen. The noise hadn't come from the back door this time which didn't surprise me. A local building supplier had donated this door which was sturdy and couldn't be kicked in as easily as the old one. Then I heard the noise again. One of the windows. Someone was trying to get in through the window next to the door.

The windows were old and although they were locked, how hard could it be to get one open? I found out when the sound of breaking glass shattered the silence.

I needed a place to hide. The closet in which we kept the cleaning supplies and whose door was warped and so never closed completely was two steps away. I inched my way to it. Noiselessly I moved the bucket and mop out of the way to get in. There wasn't much room with the stepladder leaning against the wall but I managed to crawl behind it. I pulled a couple of aprons from their hooks to cover myself, hoping I'd look like a heap of rags.

Because the door was open its usual couple of inches I could hear the intruder. He stumbled over something and cursed volubly. From the sound of his voice and the creaking of the middle drawer of my desk where I kept the bills, the account books, and the sign-in sheets of our clients, I knew where he was. What did he hope to find in the desk? Surely he didn't expect to find cash there?

I peeked out from under the aprons. I saw light beams cut through the darkness. A flashlight. When the light moved closer I pulled the aprons back over myself. I pretended to fuse into the linoleum. From this position my eyes were even with the floor.

The door opened wider. The beam of light flashed briefly into the closet. Apparently he saw nothing of interest and turned away. That's when I saw his feet. Big feet wearing sturdy black boots. I heard him walk away, heard the crunch of glass from the broken window under his boots, heard a grunt as he heaved himself through the window, and heard the window being pulled down.

I counted to a hundred before I crawled out of

the closet and punched in Uncle Barney's cell phone number. He answered immediately.

"Uncle Barney, where are you?"

"On my way to the shelter. Cybil, why are you whispering? I can hardly hear you."

"Because the intruder was just here."

"What?"

"He's gone now. I hid behind the cleaning equipment in the closet."

"I'm only a block away. Stay hidden."

"Okay. Knock twice on the door so I know it's you."

"Don't hang up. Hum so I know you're okay."

"Hum?"

"Recite a poem. Or just talk. Something to stay in touch."

For the life of me I couldn't remember a single line of poetry. That made me realize how scared I'd been and still was. So I hummed the tune of the first Christmas carol that popped into my mind. One that had noel in the refrain. That reminded me that I hadn't done any Christmas shopping but I was so not in the mood for buying presents. This was my first Christmas without my little boy. I didn't know how I was going to survive this holiday.

Before melancholy could wrap its gray constricting wings around me I heard Uncle Barney's knocks and rushed to the door.

"Cybil, it's me."

I unlocked the door. "I'm so glad to see you." I shook my head. "That has to be the understatement of the year," I admitted. Uncle Barney hugged me.

"You're okay?"

"Yes."

"Let's sit down, and you can tell me all about it."

I did. When I'd related the important facts, I asked, "Why do you suppose he bothered to close the window when he left?"

"Because an open window in midwinter would catch the eye of anyone passing by, including the patrol car that drives past here. In the dark they might not see that a pane is busted, but they would notice the open window and investigate. He needed time to get away. Our intruder is a careful planner."

"But what was he after?" I wondered out loud.

"He searched your desk. Why don't you look to see if anything's missing."

"There's nothing of value in the desk."

"Look anyway."

It wasn't until I looked in the deep drawer that something struck me as being different. Uncle Barney noticed my puzzled expression.

"What?"

"The drawer's not full enough. It's usually filled to the top, and unless I put the ledgers and sign-in books in the drawer just right, I can't even close it."

"Sign-in books?"

"Yes. I put all the sign-in sheets into three-ring binders."

"How are the binders labeled?"

"By date. Usually three months' worth of sheets fit into a binder."

"Check to see if any are missing."

I did. "The October and November sheets are missing." I looked at Uncle Barney in total confusion. "Who could possibly be interested in who stayed in the shelter those two months?"

"That's the question of the hour." He thought for a moment. "Is there any other way to determine who stayed here?"

"No. Except since it's gotten cold, our clientele hasn't changed much. So who's been here this month was probably here in November. Possibly in October as well."

"Where are the December sign-in sheets?"

"In the dining room."

"Let's have a look at them. Or better yet, let's photocopy the pages. Since we're in the first part of December, there won't be that many pages."

"Okay." I went and fetched the sheets. "The drugstore downtown is open till ten and they have a copy machine."

"I'll take them to the office in the morning and have Lynn make copies." Barney folded the sheets carefully and put them into his coat pocket. "Did you notice anything about the intruder? I know it was dark and the only light—"

"The flashlight. After he'd shone the light into the closet, he turned around and stood there for a moment. His hand holding the flashlight hung down and shone on his boot. He has big feet. Really big which suggests he's a big guy, doesn't it?"

Barney nodded.

"And the boots were black. Leather." I closed my eyes to visualize them better. "There was a strap across the instep which had silver-looking studs hammered into it. Well, it probably wasn't silver but a metal that looked like it. The boots might have been custom-made. They looked expensive."

"Very good," Barney said. "I wonder if the intruder is a member of a motorcycle club?"

"Because of the boots?"

"I know that's typecasting, but we have so little to go on that we might as well check it out."

"I didn't even know we had motorcycle clubs."

"One that I know of. I'll make inquiries."

"You know, the more I think of it, the more I'm convinced this guy is the same one who wore the ski mask and busted the door."

Barney nodded. "The thought occurred to me too."

"But why take the sign-in sheets?"

"He could be looking for someone."

"But most of our clients go by their street names or use only their first names."

"Maybe that's all he knows them by."

"I suppose I should call the police and report the intruder." When Uncle Barney nodded, I did.

A patrol car stopped at the shelter a few minutes later. The officer asked the usual questions and looked at the broken window. He said he'd send a fingerprint man in the morning, but I told him that this would not be necessary. The hand holding the flashlight had worn a black leather glove.

The officer helped Uncle Barney nail boards over the broken window.

"Miss, you should be thinking about getting an alarm system installed," he said.

I glanced at the patrolman's young face and stopped myself from sarcastically asking where he thought a shelter for the homeless was going to get money for an alarm system. He looked as if he'd just graduated from the academy, and he meant well. There was no need to antagonize him. Besides, I just might need him again.

When the window was securely nailed shut he drove off.

I was reluctant to see him leave. What if the big guy came back and broke the other windows?

I sighed. "We really don't have money to keep repairing doors and windows." And we didn't have the money to buy the metal bars for the windows I was beginning to think we needed. Some days I felt as if Abby and I were holding this shelter together with bits of mending tape and prayers and hopeless optimism.

"We'll catch the guy. It's only a matter of time," Barney said.

He patted my arm and walked me to my car. He waited until I'd started my engine before he got into his car. I followed him to the parking lot exit. He pulled out into the street but I had to wait for a pickup to pass.

There was no reason for me to look into the rear-view mirror but I did. For a moment I saw a large, dark-clad figure silhouetted against the snowy background. Alarmed, I turned for a better look. My foot slipped off the brake, causing my car to lurch forward. I slammed on the brake, causing my car to skid and make a one-hundred-and-eighty-degree turn. By the time I looked around again, there was no one there.

Had there been?

NINE

NEXT MORNING I WAS SURE that I'd imagined the large, hulking figure, so I decided not to mention it to Uncle Barney when I got to the agency. Nor did I have a chance to do so.

"Lieutenant Keller wants to talk to you," Lynn informed me frostily the moment I opened the agency door. "He called two times already."

She held up two fingers to be sure I got the point.

"I'll call him."

"No. He wants to see you in his office. What you do this time?" she demanded, her eyes suspicious.

"I found a dead body."

"That's bad karma. Very bad karma."

It seemed to me all my karma had been bad for a long time. I saw the sign-in sheets and the photocopies on her desk, stacked in neat piles.

"I have to return the originals to the shelter," I said, holding out my hand. She hesitated. "Oh, for heaven's sake. Ask Uncle Barney if you don't believe me."

Lynn handed them to me, which suggested that she'd already checked with Uncle Barney.

I laid the sheets on the back seat of my car before

I walked to the police department. Sam's office door was open so I walked in. When he saw me he hastily dropped something in the open desk drawer.

"Sneaking snacks again," I said and sat down.

"I don't know what gave you that idea…"

"Could it be the cookie crumbs on your tie?"

Sam hastily brushed them off.

"If you're going to cheat on you diet with something sweet, Oma's *Lebkuchen* are definitely the least harmful to your cholesterol level. Their fat content isn't all that high."

"Oh yeah?" He retrieved the cookie from the drawer.

I saw that it was a *Lebkuchen*. "They also contain almonds, which are good for you."

His blue eyes lit up as if I'd just given him a great present. He finished the cookie. "Lynn told me you wanted to see me?"

"Why didn't you tell me that Margot Chesterton Dowd was in the club when her husband was stabbed?"

Taken aback, I blinked. "I didn't see her *in* the club. Just on the back road *near* the club. Who says she was in the club?"

"One of the maintenance guys."

"How does he know her? They don't exactly move in the same circles."

"No, but he's seen her picture in the paper, and he noticed her snazzy car."

"The silver Avanti wasn't in the club's parking lot. Did you check with the gatekeeper? I bet he didn't see it."

Sam's eyes narrowed. "Were you the female voice from the front office that sent him looking for the car?"

I shrugged, trying to look enigmatic. "Did he see her car?"

"No, but he thinks he saw her."

"Thinks?"

Sam shrugged.

"She didn't drive into the club with her husband, so how did she get in?"

"Maybe the same way you did. Sneaked in."

I considered that for a moment before I shook my head. "She's one of the richest and most powerful women in town. She's not used to sneaking into any place."

"You think the rich can't be sneaky?" Sam asked, his tone incredulous.

"I'm sure they can in their own way." I tried to picture the coolly elegant woman sneaking into a place she was used to driving in unchallenged. I couldn't. "No, I can't see her doing it."

"And yet the maintenance man is pretty sure he saw her."

I shook my head.

"From what I've heard about her husband, she had plenty of provocation to do him in," Sam said.

"Are you considering the holy trio of means, opportunity, and motive?"

"Works every time," Sam maintained.

"Not in this case. Since no one can place her at the scene with certainty, opportunity is questionable. Means? A knife was used. The kind you can find in any kitchen. I'm sure I have one very much like it. And motive?"

"It's usually love or money," Sam said. "Or if you want to be a little more crass, lust or lucre. Or any variation of the two."

"You can rule out money. She has lots more than he has. Had."

"Well, that leaves love or lust."

"According to the grapevine at the office, Ron's had affairs for years and it's doubtful that his wife was unaware of them. She didn't do anything about them."

"Maybe she ran out of patience. Maybe she said enough is enough. Maybe he got serious about one of the women and—"

"No." I shook my head again. "Not when he took out at least two different women. Have you interviewed the two I told you about?"

"Yup."

"And?"

"I can't talk about them. They're part of an ongoing investigation."

I looked at him in exasperation. "When it suits

your purpose *not* to talk about something it becomes part of an investigation."

Sam grinned at me. "That's one of the perks of the badge."

I stood. "Did you locate anyone who saw who it was sneaking out the emergency door?"

"No."

"Then it must have been somebody who blends in to the club scene. A regular guest or an employee." I turned to go when I remembered something. "Did you find out why the alarm didn't go off?"

"Yup. It was disconnected. The manager swears that they check the alarm system regularly so somebody switched it off deliberately."

"Is that hard to do?"

"Not if you can read TURN OFF and follow the arrow showing the direction," Sam said.

"That certainly doesn't narrow down the list of suspects."

"Sure doesn't," he agreed. "What about the money part of the motive?"

"Margot Chesterton Dowd has more money than she can spend in several lifetimes. She doesn't need his assets." At least not his financial assets. As to his assets as a husband and lover—I stopped myself. Margot was our client and therefore above suspicion.

"If we rule out money, you know what that leaves: love and its accompanying emotions such as jealousy, possessiveness, resentment, obsession. Even an understanding, forgiving spouse can snap suddenly."

"You're bound and determined to pin this murder on our client?"

"So far she looks best for it."

I didn't like the sound of that. "Have you looked at the business angle? Could be a business rival."

"We'll take a look but it doesn't appear promising."

I hated to ask but I had to know. "What about the tire tracks at the club on the day of Ron's murder?"

"Unfortunately by the time we got to them other cars had driven over them. I don't suppose you can look at pictures of tire tracks and identify them?"

I merely gave him a long look.

"Just thought I'd ask."

I took my leave and rushed back to the agency to talk to Uncle Barney but he wasn't there. Disappointed, I went to my office upstairs.

When the building had been a private residence, my office must have been a bedroom. Maxi sensed a feminine aura in the room and could picture a four-poster bed and ruffled, fluffy curtains over the windows.

I watered my plants which crowded the two deep window sills. They looked great thanks to Maxi's advice on when to feed and water them. The schefflera had grown big and probably would need to be repotted soon.

Sitting at my desk, I summarized everything I knew about the Ron Dowd case. Glenn came in. I jumped up and hugged him.

"Aren't you supposed to be home in bed?" I asked.

"I'm getting cabin fever. Had to get out. I'm feeling good. What's happening?"

I invited him to sit down and asked him to listen to my summary.

"Ron's wife hires us to follow him. We do so and discover that he's got women on the side. Employees, no less. We also found out that something is going on between him and Frederick Holmes. Something that isn't entirely friendly and from the look of that envelope, involves money. And then Ron is found stabbed to death at the club."

Glenn nodded. "A club to which both Frederick and Margot have access but not the girls from the secretarial pool."

"Yes, but they could have sneaked in. I did."

"But you're a lot sneakier and smarter than they are."

"Thank you, I think."

Glenn grinned at me. Then he grew serious. "All this is going to be academic anyway."

"Why?"

"It's now a police matter. What do you want to bet that Mrs. Dowd will send a check and tell us we're off the case? Her cheating hubby is dead. She doesn't need a divorce now. Someone took care of him for her."

We looked at each other. I shook my head. "She couldn't have hired someone to stab him."

"Probably not. It's a lot harder to find a hit man than the movies lead you to believe."

"And she couldn't have stabbed him herself."

"Why not?" Glenn asked, his voice challenging.

"Because…"

"Don't tell me it's because she's a woman."

"No, because it doesn't fit her image."

"That's lame, Cybil. I talked to some people. She has a reputation for being one tough cookie."

"Just because she's tough in business doesn't mean she's capable of plunging a knife into her husband's chest."

"True. And she's our client."

His sigh sounded regretful. My intercom buzzed. I picked up the phone. Uncle Barney wanted to see us.

It turned out that we were still on the job.

"Uncle Barney, does Mrs. Dowd really think we can find out who killed her husband before the police do?"

"She's afraid that she's their main suspect and that they won't look hard for anyone else."

"She has a point," Glenn said.

"How strong is her alibi?" I asked.

"So-so. She says she was at home later that morning," Barney said.

"Except I saw her follow her husband. She didn't go into the club, at least I didn't see her do it, but she was there."

"She doesn't deny that. She was planning to go to the club but changed her mind. She turned around and drove home."

"Anyone at home to verify that?" Glenn asked.

"No. The maid had the day off," Barney said. "It's our job to find at least one alternative suspect that her attorney can use to create reasonable doubt. She doesn't have to prove her innocence. The prosecutor has to prove her guilt."

I was familiar with the concept.

"So we're looking for someone else who had reason to kill Ron Dowd or who would profit by his death," Glenn summarized.

"That about covers it," Barney said and dismissed us.

I hastened to the Chesterton offices and Glenn to the club.

THE SUPERVISOR ASSIGNED me to work in the main office in which six women had their work stations. My desk was next to Kelli's. A stroke of luck.

Flicking furtive glances at her I saw that she looked ill. The third time she ran to the ladies' room I followed her. I turned the water on not so much because I needed to wash my hands as to drown out the retching sounds from one of the stalls. I wanted to give Kelli a little privacy.

When she came out to splash water on her face, I handed her a paper towel. She took it and nodded her thanks.

"Morning sickness is the pits, isn't it?" I said softly.

She tottered as if I'd hit her.

"You can tell? I'm already showing?" She glanced down her skirt.

"No, you're not, but I remember throwing up like that when I was pregnant. How far along are you?"

"Three months."

"The father of the baby? Is he in the picture?"

Kelli's face crumpled and she began to weep. I called myself seven kinds of a fool for being so direct. Still, she needed to talk to someone. She needed help.

I pulled a couple of tissues from the box on the counter and handed them to her. "I used to be a social worker. I know how you can get relatively inexpensive prenatal care and help after the baby's born. That is, if you're going to keep it."

Kelli stopped crying and looked at me wide-eyed. "I'm going to keep the baby. How can I give it up? I loved him so."

More tears. "Is he willing to help?" I asked, knowing full well he couldn't.

"He's dead," she whispered and sobbed heart-breakingly.

I let her weep a while. Then I handed her my card. "Call me and I'll give you the information about the prenatal clinic. Don't wait. You need proper care if you want your baby to be born strong and healthy."

She nodded. "Thanks."

"How are you fixed for money? I know agencies—"

"I know how I can get what I need," she said, her voice hard.

I returned to my desk. A few minutes later so did Kelli, looking wan and beaten down.

Sitting at my desk I kept thinking about her. Had Ron promised her marriage? Had he even known about the baby? Had he promised to get a divorce? Of course, she hadn't come right out and said the father was Ron.

I kept an eye on her but she held it together until lunch time when she looked at something in her desk drawer that caused her to burst into silent tears before she rushed from the room.

The secretaries headed for the lunch room. As soon as their voices faded I went to Kelli's desk and opened her middle drawer. Under a manila folder I found a snapshot of Ron Dowd. "You cheating louse," I muttered and slammed the drawer shut.

In the lunch room I retrieved my brown paper sack from the fridge and joined Debbie.

"I see you remembered to bring your lunch," she said.

"Yes. Peanut butter and banana on nine grain bread."

"Sounds good." She took a bite from her ham sandwich before she spoke. "You heard what happened to Mr. Dowd?"

"Yes. What's the grapevine saying?"

Debbie shrugged. "Nobody knows anything for sure but we suspect it has something to do with his tomcatting. Maybe some boyfriend or husband got tired of him poaching and took him out."

"Any candidates?"

"Well, the cops talked to Kelli. I don't know if it was because she was his secretary or because she'd been seeing Ron. But I don't think she had a serious boyfriend who stabbed her lover in a fit of jealousy."

"Does she have an alibi?"

"I don't know but the cops haven't arrested her. Besides, she's not tough enough to stab a guy."

Just then Margot Chesterton Dowd passed the lunch room door. "Now there's a strong, tough woman," Debbie said admiringly. "When the security guard caught one of the secretaries stealing office supplies, Mrs. Dowd fired her on the spot. Over a box of paperclips and a half dozen number two pencils." Debbie shook her head.

I hated to think what our client would do to one of her employees who threatened to steal her husband.

I found myself hoping she wouldn't find out about Kelli. The girl had enough problems.

MAXI CAME DOWN WITH a bad cold and cough which Luke feared might turn into bronchitis, so he ordered bed rest. Maxi fretted about her St. Nicholas luncheon until my mother jumped in and offered to hold an open house that evening instead.

This was the second social occasion I would have to attend at her mansion in a month, and I wasn't thrilled about it. Still, I couldn't think of a good way to get out of it so I went. I even bought a new dress. On sale, naturally, as it was doubtful I'd have another occasion to wear a cocktail dress that had practically no back, not unless you wanted to count a couple of thin straps.

As always, Mom's catered buffet was lavish. As I looked over the selections, Luke joined me.

"Your mother certainly knows how to throw a party," he said, placing several items on his plate. "What are those?"

"Miniature puff pastries stuffed with crab salad. They're delicious. You should try them."

Luke popped one into his mouth. "They are good," he agreed, and placed several on his plate.

I reached for a spring roll and smoked salmon curled atop a slice of cucumber. "The only problem with this kind of food is that you either leave hungry and have to get a hamburger on the way home or you leave the table looking like a swarm of locusts hit it."

"Tell you what. We'll be polite and just nibble and then we'll stop for burgers. My treat. I owe you for those cookies you baked. All my favorites."

I flicked him an amused glanced. "Is there a cookie that isn't your favorite?"

"Not any that you or Maxi bake."

"Thank you but you're just used to ours."

"Wrong. I am a cookie expert and can differentiate between the excellent, the mediocre, and the awful."

"That sounds like the title of a spaghetti western."

Luke smiled at that. The tired look I'd noticed disappeared. "You always could make me smile," he said.

I turned from the table. A soft, appreciative whistle stopped me. "What?"

"That's a great dress, even if the designer forgot to sew the back on. Or because of it. Shows off your swimmer's muscles. Your back is magnificently toned. Makes a man's fingers itch to caress it."

Though it was flattering to hear Luke's compliment, it was also dangerous. I knew how susceptible I was to his low, seductive voice.

"Thank you," I said lightly. "You want some of this?" I held out the relish tray.

"No, that's not what I want, and you know it."

Fortunately, Sam joined us. "Anything substantial on the table, cuz?" he asked after greeting us.

"On my mom's buffet? You should know better than to ask."

"A man can hope."

"Try those little biscuits stuffed with ham," Luke said.

Sam picked up the platter and slid the little sandwiches onto his plate. "What?" he asked, looking at me.

"I didn't say a thing."

"Knowing your mom, the caterer will have more of these in the kitchen."

The three of us withdrew to a corner.

"Any news on the deaths at the shelter?" Luke asked.

"No. We canvassed every craft shop in town and no one has a record of selling castor beans."

"Which suggests that they were bought somewhere else or that the person had them for a craft's project," I said.

"Or had access to someone who does crafts," Sam added.

"How many women in Westport are into crafts?" Luke wondered.

"In a small town, probably half of the over fifty crowd does some sort of handwork," I said. "How else could we keep three craft shops in business?"

"So, the castor beans are pretty much a dead end," Luke said.

"You've talked to the owner of the Aces High Club and the Reverend Brown?" I asked.

Sam nodded. "Both want the building but not enough to commit multiple murders."

"How about the Maniac Messiah?"

Sam made a twirling motion with his finger. "Squirrelier than a dozen squirrels."

"You don't think anyone mentally unbalanced can kill?" Luke asked.

"Anyone can kill," Sam said. "The difference is only in how. I can picture Maniac hearing a voice telling him to make a sacrifice, like Abraham in the Bible, but get a hold of castor beans and plot the killing carefully and cunningly? No. Way too spaced out for that."

Sam sounded so convinced that he convinced me as well.

I was tempted to leave the party then but that was a bit too much like eating and running. Looking around the crowd I saw that Frederick Holmes and his wife had arrived. I waited until Frederick was deeply into a conversation with some businessmen, with Brittany standing there trying not to look bored to death, before I approached her.

"Want to share my plate of carrot sticks and celery? I know a place where we can sit and talk." She followed me to my stepfather's den. We sat on its leather sofa.

Brittany took a celery stick. "If I have to eat one more piece of fruitcake and drink one more cup of eggnog, I'll start screaming."

"I know what you mean." I got up and took two bottles of water from the little fridge my stepfather kept in the credenza. I handed her one.

"If I have to go to many more holiday parties I'll have to start going to the gym twice a day," she said. 'How does your mother stay so slim? I see her at every party."

"She worked out a system. Places a few things on her plate. Nibbles on the celery sticks or cucumbers. Never carrots because bits stick between your teeth." We both ran our tongue over our teeth. "Eventually she ditches the plate, virtually untouched. She nurses the one drink she allows herself. Usually something like a gin and tonic which she has the waiter refill with just diet tonic."

"Smart," Brittany said. "From now on, it's G-and-T for me too."

"Wine spritzers work well too."

"What do you do?" she asked.

"I'm not embarrassed to ask for straight tomato juice." Changing the subject I asked, "How are your stepsons? You were concerned about Cameron's weight gains. How's he doing?"

Brittany sighed. "He doesn't talk to me much. But

the good thing is that he's walking. Several times he's left the house on foot and returned the same way. He's never done that before. He's acting weird. Even for him."

"Where do you suppose he walks to?"

She lifted her shoulders in a shrug. "I don't know. He walks at night but as long as he walks I don't care where he goes. He's got a part-time job and he's been helping his dad in the nursery, which is also something new. Frederick tells me Cameron has no trouble handling the Christmas trees people plan to plant after the holidays."

When I looked puzzled, she explained.

"The ones where the roots are dug up with a big ball of soil around them. They're wrapped in burlap. They must weight over a hundred pounds."

"Oh yes. I've seen those."

"What kind of tree did you put up?" Brittany asked.

"I haven't yet." I didn't add that I couldn't bear to put up a tree, that I was afraid the memories of last Christmas with my sweet little boy might cause me to totally fall apart. Changing the subject, I asked, "And how do you fill your days?"

"Promise you won't laugh if I tell you?"

"I won't," I promised.

"At one of the parties I admired some needlepoint pillows in the hostess's home. She told me she took classes at The Happy Needle, which is a craft store on Main Street. She talked me into taking a class there, too, and I got hooked on doing needlepoint."

"That's great. I used to do quite a bit of knitting and found it very relaxing. I should take it up again."

Frederick came to claim Brittany to introduce her to a business contact.

I stayed only long enough not to offend my mother. I sneaked out, as I wasn't in the mood to go for hamburgers with Luke. I should have told him but thinking of Ryan and then being with his father might be too much. Better leave and concentrate on the present and on business.

On the way home I remembered that I hadn't taken out the sausage patties from the freezer for tomorrow's breakfast, so I headed toward the shelter.

The light above the kitchen door was out again. Blast. I'd have to find a better brand of light bulbs that lasted longer than two weeks. I unlocked the door and entered. Before I could close it and turn on the light, someone grabbed me from behind. I managed to let out one good scream before a gloved hand clamped itself over my mouth. I kicked backward. The grunt that followed told me that my kick had connected forcefully. In retaliation his huge hand closed around my throat and squeezed.

I struggled to raise my arms and slip them between his forearm and my neck. Pressing hard, I forced him to loosen his grip. I gulped in air and wondered how long my strength would last. Not long. My arms started to tremble.

"Let her go."

Glenn's voice. I heard a thud. My attacker grunted and loosened his hold on me some more. I saw his bare wrist between his coat sleeve and his glove and sank my teeth into it hard. He yelped and released me. From behind, Glenn hit him again with the snow shovel. I grabbed the broom I had left beside the door and whacked him as hard as I could. Facing two weapon-wielding defenders, he pushed Glenn back and ran past him.

I grabbed Glenn, pulled him inside, and slammed the door behind us and locked it. Then, leaning against it, I slid to the floor. Glenn collapsed beside me. In the silence I heard nothing but our rasping, gasping breaths.

"You okay?" Glenn asked.

"Yes. You? Sure you didn't rip your stitches?"

"Yeah." He took a few breaths before he spoke again. "Who is that big ape, and what does he want here?"

"I have no idea but I think we better call the cops."

I felt around the floor for the purse I'd dropped when he had grabbed me. I found it and my cell phone and dialed 911.

We sat on the floor until we heard the siren of the approaching police car.

The same young cop arrived and started to take

our statements. Moments later Sam burst through the door.

"I thought I left you at Mom's party," I said.

"You did, but when I got the news of your nine-one-one call…"

"Why did they inform you of my call?"

"Because I asked them to."

Just then Luke and Uncle Barney rushed in.

"I sure emptied Mom's party," I said. "She couldn't be happy about that."

"There were enough people there that she hardly noticed," Luke said.

"Tell me what happened," Sam said.

"There isn't much to tell. I had just unlocked the door when that big guy grabbed me. I yelled and I guess Glenn heard me."

Glenn nodded. "I did and smacked the guy with the snow shovel that we keep outside the kitchen door."

"Did the attacker say anything?"

"He sort of yelped when I bit his wrist."

"You bit him?" Sam asked.

"Yes. He was choking me." My voice sounded defensive. I fingered my neck, which Luke insisted on examining while Glenn finished the story.

"You're going to be bruised," Luke said, gently touching my throat.

"Did either of you get a good look at him?" Sam asked.

"No. He was wearing a ski mask."

"So, he's the same big guy who was here before?"

"Yes, Uncle Barney. Which means he still hasn't gotten whatever it is he's looking for."

Barney examined the window facing the alley. The crunching of glass under his shoes told us that's how he got into the shelter.

I groaned. "Not again. We simply don't have the budget to keep replacing window panes."

"My Christmas present to you and the shelter will be steel bars for those windows," Luke announced, his expression grim.

"Good idea." Sam nodded approvingly. "I'll send the fingerprint man over in the morning."

"Don't bother. He wore leather gloves."

"That guy is really beginning to annoy me," Sam muttered.

He helped Uncle Barney nail boards over the window while I removed sausage patties for tomorrow's breakfast.

TEN

GLENN'S PHONE CALL woke me at seven the next morning.

"You better get over here. To the club."

"Why? What happened?" I pulled the down comforter up to my neck. The room was cold.

"Something you need to hear. Drive around to the back of the locker room building."

"I'll be there as soon as I can." I splashed water on my face, brushed my teeth, and pulled my hair into a ponytail. Then I dressed warmly in record speed. My single-cup coffeemaker brewed a fragrant cup while I fed Buddy. Five minutes later I was on my way, sipping strong, black coffee from a travel mug.

It hadn't snowed during the night so the roads were clear and I made good time.

Glenn and a fortysomething guy with longish brown hair under a knit cap waited in Glenn's pickup. They got out as I approached.

"Cybil, this is Louis. He's one of the maintenance men here at the club. Well, right now he's the only one."

"Hi, Louis. That's a lot of work for one man," I said, looking around.

"You got that right," he said, aggrieved. "Can't seem to keep help. Especially the young ones. The work day's too long for them."

I nodded sympathetically.

"Tell Cybil what you told me. About that day."

"What day?" I asked.

"The day they found that guy stabbed. Only at the time I didn't know nothing about that."

"What happened that day?" I asked.

"After clearing the walkways, I came back for a cup of coffee. Brought my thermos from home," Louis explained. "There was this guy wearing coveralls like mine."

He pointed to his beige coveralls which had the club's name stitched over his left breast pocket.

"Only they were too big on him, you know? Had the pant legs and sleeves rolled up."

"So, he was short?"

"Yeah. Maybe your height," Louis said, looking at me.

At five-foot-five I had never thought of myself as short, but I guess it was all a matter of perspective.

"What did he look like?" Glenn asked.

"At first I thought he was just a kid. Short and skinny. Then I saw his face for a moment and he had lines around his eyes and on his forehead."

"What color was his hair?" I asked.

"He wore a cap, but what I saw of it his hair was brown. More light brown than dark."

"And the color of his eyes?" I had to pry out each piece of information as if I were pulling teeth.

Louis shrugged. "He wore tinted glasses. I couldn't tell what color his eyes were. I only saw his face for a moment."

"Anything else?" I asked.

"Yeah. He walked funny."

"Funny? How?" I asked.

Louis shrugged. "Short steps. Kinda graceful."

Glenn nodded. "Go on."

"He went into the garage," he said, pointing at the building behind him, "and I went to sit in my truck and drank coffee."

"Had you ever seen this guy before?" I asked.

"No. I thought maybe they'd hired him to help me, but since I ain't seen him since I guess they didn't. Or he quit."

"But you did see the silver Avanti?" I asked.

"Well, not seen it. I was shoveling snow when I heard it."

"Heard it?" I asked, my tone a bit skeptical.

"Yeah. It has a special sound. If you know cars you can often recognize them by their sounds."

"Where do you think the Avanti you heard was?"

"Only place it could have been. Back there in the garage where we keep our vehicles."

"Did you check the garage that morning?" Glenn asked.

"Had no reason to. The snowplow was out here,

and I went straight to work clearing the roads and walkways."

Glenn and I looked at each other. Neither one of us could think of anything else to ask Louis. We thanked him and walked away.

"I checked with the office. The woman who does the hiring is on vacation. The girl who's filling in for her is pretty sure they haven't hired anybody recently. This helper could be the killer. Or he could have seen the killer," Glenn said.

"Has to be the killer. Why else would anyone masquerade as a maintenance man?" I wondered out loud.

"Maybe I should talk to this Kelli. Maybe she didn't tell you about a jealous boyfriend—"

"No jealous boyfriend," I said quickly. But I hadn't asked about an outraged father or brother who hated the married man who got her pregnant. But how could he have gotten into the club? *Dumb question, Cybil.* If I could get in anyone could. "I'll talk to her again." I had planned to anyway.

Then I asked the question that really bothered me. "Why would Margot Chesterton Dowd drive her car into this garage?"

"Yeah. Makes no sense. Unless she didn't want anyone to see her here at the club."

"And how did she get into the club? The gatekeeper doesn't remember her. Unless..."

"Unless?" Glenn prompted.

"Unless she somehow got a key to unlock the gate to the back entrance? We need to find out how she got it." I thought for a moment. "Most likely bribed somebody."

"We're supposed to find other suspects for the murder, not get our client deeper into trouble," Glenn said.

I nodded. "But what if she—"

"I know. Let's rule out everyone else first before we even consider her."

"Okay. Let's see who else there is." I thought for a second. "Frederick Holmes and Ron. What was going on between them?" I asked.

"Good question. You saw money change hands?"

"Yes. A tidy sum, judging by the thickness of the envelope." I paused, thinking. "You think Margot will let us look at her husband's financial records?"

"Doubtful." Glenn paced. When he stopped, he said, "Can you stay late at the office tomorrow night?"

"I suppose so. Why?"

"We need to take a look at Ron's desk. Has anybody taken his place yet?" Glenn asked.

"The man hasn't even been buried yet," I said, shocked.

"Oh, right. I'll get into the building and join you around five-thirty. By then everyone should have gone home."

By 4:55 WHEN ALL THE women had backed up their computers, I went into the restroom and stayed there for ten minutes. When I got back to the office everyone had left. Funny how quickly a whole floor could be emptied. I sat at my desk and worked on a crossword puzzle while waiting for Glenn.

When I heard the office door opening I turned expectantly, but it was only two custodians wheeling their equipment cart. Then it hit me and I turned around again. Glenn, wearing gray pants and matching shirt, grinned at me.

"This is Emil," he said, introducing his companion.

I shook hands with Emil.

"He's a computer expert. We thought we might take a look at Ron's computer."

"But that's illegal," I blurted out. "At least I think it is."

"So is murder and that I know for a fact," Glenn said. "Which was Ron's office?"

I pointed.

"Okay. You stay out here and keep watch. If anyone comes have a sneezing fit."

"A sneezing fit? I can't sneeze on command."

"Then have a coughing fit. Ask whoever comes in to get you some water. That'll warn us and give us a chance to get out."

Five nerve-wrecking minutes later I discovered that under this kind of tension I wasn't good at waiting. My hands shook. I swiveled my chair so that I could see the main entrance to the office. Any minute I expected the real custodian to come in and demand to know how his cart got into the office. What could I say? My mind went blank.

I kept taking deep breaths to calm myself. I stared at the crossword puzzle but couldn't even think of the four-letter word for the god of love.

When the men came out of Ron's office Emil carried a floppy disk. "We made a copy," Glenn explained. "Faster and safer. Stay exactly four minutes to give us a chance to get out of the building before you leave."

"Shall we synchronize our watches?" Emil asked with a grin.

How could he joke at a time like this? Nevertheless, I checked my watch as they left. To be on the safe side I waited an extra thirty seconds before I left, not exactly running, but walking awfully fast. I made up a number of excuses I could use to explain staying late should anyone ask me. No one did. Actually, no one even saw me.

I drove straight to the agency, where Emil was staring at computer screen. Glenn sat at his desk reading the sports page of today's paper.

"Anything yet?" I asked him in a low voice.

Glenn shook his head and placed a finger over his lips. I got the message and sat down. He handed me the food section of the paper. There was an interesting recipe for roasted winter vegetables. I wasn't terribly fond of beets, but roasted with parsnips, onions, garlic, carrots, Yukon gold potatoes, rosemary, and olive oil, they sounded quite good. I cut out the recipe and placed it into my purse.

"Aha!"

We both looked at Emil. What did *aha* mean in computerese? Emil didn't say anything else and since Glenn, who knew him, remained silent, so did I.

After a while Emil spoke. "The subject kept a separate and probably secret account of his personal money. Labeled it LAUNDRY and DRY CLEANING. Can you believe that? Hadn't he ever heard of money laundering?" Emil chuckled and shook his head.

"What should he have named it?" I asked, intrigued.

"Something he was familiar with. Something routine in his life. He liked sports. I doubt anyone would have opened a file labeled GOLF. Who'd be interested in his golf scores?"

Emil was undoubtedly right. Ron hadn't been the sharpest knife in the drawer but that didn't justify someone depriving him of his life. If I had a secret computer file, what would I name it? Cats? Flowers? Probably too obvious. Glenn's question rescued me from my speculations.

"Can you open the file?"

Emil shot him a pitying look, let his fingers fly

over the keyboard and moments later columns of figures appeared on the screen.

"Hmm, doesn't look like regular, legitimate income. No notations of the source of the money, no receipts. Just dates, initials, and amounts."

"Blackmail?" Glenn asked.

I looked at the initials for the day I had followed Ron to the nursery. Sure enough there was the date, the initials FH, and $5,000. Frederick Holmes had paid Ron $5,000. I wish I knew what for.

"Probably blackmail," I agreed. "I know who FH is but not the others. Can we get printed copies of this?"

Emil typed in a command and moments later we had copies of the printouts.

Glenn thanked Emil and reminded him to send the agency a bill.

As I studied the list of blackmail victims, I discovered the initials JM. My heart skipped a beat. Justin Merriweather? My stepfather? Since I couldn't imagine the man whom I secretly thought of as bland as instant pudding doing anything that was worthy of blackmail I dismissed the idea. The letters JM could stand for a hundred different combinations of names.

"Well, we've just discovered a bunch of people with motives for murdering Ron," Glenn said.

"Maybe, but blackmail doesn't necessarily lead to murder."

"No, but the blackmailed victims can either run

out of money or get tired of being bled dry and take action," he said. "Why do you suppose a guy like Ron Dowd would stoop to blackmail?"

"In his case, money," I said without hesitation. "Remember he had only his salary, no independent wealth."

Glenn blew a heartfelt raspberry. "His salary would make most of us feel rich."

"True, but he had expensive habits. Golf is not a cheap sport and then all those girlfriends he had to wine and dine."

"You think the Westport PD looked at Ron's computer?" Glenn asked.

"I can't imagine why they wouldn't have. I'm going to call Sam. Maybe he'll let something slip."

I did and my cousin assured me they'd looked at the computer.

"Did you find anything interesting"

"Sure did. Sources of unusual income."

"Such as?"

"Cybil, you know I can't tell you that."

"By unusual I take it you mean illegal? Such as gambling? Blackmailing? Cheating on income tax? Fraud of some sort?"

"Why did you include blackmail in your list?"

"Because I can't see Ron committing any ordinary crimes such as breaking and entering, stealing cars, robbing banks. It would have to be a gentleman's crime."

Sam chuckled. I could picture him shaking his head.

"Gentleman's crime? There's no such thing. White collar, maybe, though to me a crime is a crime."

"Any idea whom Ron blackmailed?"

"Just initials. Cybil, if you know something, spill it."

"I don't *know* anything for sure."

"But you have your suspicions?"

"Nothing you could take to a court of law."

"Be careful. We're dealing with someone who's killed once already. Second time seems to be easier. Don't you dare put me in a position where I'd have to tell your mom and Luke, or God forbid, Maxi, that something happened to you."

"Don't worry. I'm keeping a very low profile."

"That'll be the day," he muttered before he hung up.

UNCLE BARNEY'S ORDERS were that until we caught up with the big guy stalking the shelter I could be there only if Glenn was with me. I thought this was an extreme measure to take during broad daylight, but Uncle Barney was adamant.

After my dinner shift at the shelter I had to go to the grocery store. I could get by with what I had in my pantry but Buddy, my ever-hungry kitten, needed food. Glenn, saying his fridge was sort of bare, went with me. He was right behind me in the checkout line. When I glanced at his cart my mouth dropped open.

"Is that what you're buying?" I asked before I realized what a redundant question that was.

"Well, yeah," he said, bewildered. "What's wrong with it?"

"Everything. Let's get out of this line for a minute. What happened to the cooking lessons you were going to take?"

Glenn, who'd gotten divorced six months ago, was living alone in an apartment that typically featured dishes in the kitchen sink, newspapers littering the living room floor, and discarded clothing covering every surface in the bedroom.

He shrugged, looking a little guilty. "I forgot to sign up for the winter session. But they're offering one in the spring. Beginning of March. I promise I'll do it then."

Taking my planner out of my purse, I turned to the February page and made a note to remind him. I looked at his cart and sighed. "You realize there's nothing in there from the fruit and vegetable section?"

Glenn scratched his chin, a gesture he used when he was uncomfortable, confused, or embarrassed. "I have to confess that I don't know what most of those green things are."

"I don't expect you to sauté broccoli or steam kale but how about some fresh fruit? You know, apples, bananas, pears, oranges?"

He perked up. "Oh, yeah. I like those, but I didn't see any."

"That's because you bypassed the entire produce section. Go straight back to the far end of the store. That's where they are. You might want to rethink buying four large bags of chips. They're nothing but fat and salt. Didn't you tell me that your cholesterol level was in the above-normal range at your last checkup?"

Glenn nodded glumly and set off to get fruit while I picked up one of the magazines conveniently stacked in the checkout lane and leafed through it. A few minutes later he returned, practically running, and left his cart behind mine. Then he dashed toward the exit.

"What on earth?" I muttered. I didn't even get to the front of the line before he came back, breathing hard.

"What happened?" I asked.

"I'm pretty sure I saw the big guy who's been bothering you at the shelter. I lost him but I think he was driving away in a dark Dodge Ram."

"Dark colored could be navy, forest green or black or several other shades. How many dark-colored Dodge Rams do you think there are on the road?"

"Too many. It's a popular model with guys. Still, it's one more thing we know about him that we didn't know before: the kind of vehicle he drives and that he's young. Early twenties, I'm guessing."

That didn't seem to narrow our list of suspects down a whole lot but I didn't say so.

Glenn followed me home, waiting until I was safely inside with my groceries before he drove off.

I HAD JUST FINISHED eating the chicken stirfry I'd fixed for myself when the phone rang. It was Louis from the club.

"Mrs. Quindt, I just found something you might be interested in. The coveralls."

"The coveralls?" I asked, having no idea what he was talking about.

"The coveralls the guy wore. You know, the one pretending to be a maintenance man."

I gasped. "Those! Where did you find them?"

"In the club's garage, stuck behind the lawnmowers. The only reason I had to go near the lawnmowers before next spring was that I needed to move them for the extra salt I got for the walkways."

"Clever of the killer to hide them behind equipment he had every reason to believe nobody would look at for months." Then a thought hit me. "How do you know these are the same coveralls?"

"Because the sleeves and pant legs are rolled up."

Excitement caused me to have to take an extra breath before I could speak. "Louis, leave them there and don't touch anything else. And don't let anyone else touch them. I'll be there as fast as I can. I imagine Lieutenant Keller will be there before me or right behind me. I'll call him."

As I'd anticipated, Sam was about two blocks ahead of me all the way to the club. When I arrived, he was already gloved and placing the coveralls into an evidence bag.

"I wonder how the killer got these?" Sam asked.

"I remember seeing a stack of clean ones in the laundry room. You think we'll get anything off of them?"

"Probably. The problem will be that we may not have anyone on file to compare our findings to. Still, eventually they'll be the nails for the coffin, so to speak."

Nails for the coffin? I must have looked puzzled.

"The last piece of physical evidence to convict his sorry rump," Sam explained.

"Good." I looked around the garage which at one point had been a barn. The entire club sat on a piece of property that had once been a working farm. In my opinion it had been infinitely more valuable as a farm than this overpriced playground for the affluent, but nobody had consulted me on the conversion. I hated to see acre after acre of rich farmland being covered with concrete.

Even though it was late I returned to the agency to leave a note for Uncle Barney relating what had happened.

To my surprise he was still there. He had a client in his office. I was going to tiptoe upstairs to my office but he saw me and called me in. The client turned out to be Margot Chesterton Dowd.

She had taken off her coat and tossed it negligently over the other easy chair in the office. That's how I noticed that the plain beige wool coat was lined with what had to be authentic and very expensive fur. None of the imitation fur was that glossy. I guess when you feel that you don't have to show off your fur but use it for a warm lining, that's when you're truly rich. Or someone who is afraid of tangling with the small but very vocal anti-fur protest group of Westport. Margot didn't strike me as a woman who'd be afraid of anyone.

She had kept on her fur hat which reminded me of the hats worn by important Cold War Kremlin politicians, but on her auburn hair it looked a lot better. While she listened to Uncle Barney's report, I flicked quick, assessing looks at her. From the tailored suit to the silk blouse to the high-heeled boots, she looked as if she could pose for a glossy fashion magazine.

Did she employ a personal shopper? That would make sense. I'd seen her schedule and it didn't set aside blocks of time for the kind of shopping her wardrobe necessitated.

Thinking of a personal shopper, I repressed a half-envious sigh.

"The police have now been twice to my house to question me," she said, her tone accusing.

I didn't like that she looked at Uncle Barney as if this were his fault.

"I haven't even had time to make funeral arrangements," she added resentfully.

"It'll be several days yet before the authorities will release your husband's body," Barney said. "And it's not unusual for them to question everyone several times as new facts and reports become available."

Uncle Barney's voice could be as soothing as a shaman's weaving a spell. I noticed that it even worked on Margot. She looked becalmed when she slipped into her spectacular coat a few minutes later and left, expensive perfume wafting in her wake.

Uncle Barney walked to the window, opened it a crack, and lit his pipe. He smoked in the office only when something bothered him.

"What have you found out?" he finally asked.

"That Ron Dowd was an adulterer, that most likely he was also a blackmailer who had a secret account, that someone impersonated a maintenance man at the club on that fateful morning, and that our client was at the club when she claimed to have been home."

"Now that's what I call a mixed bag of tangled blessings. Give me details."

I did, including the coveralls Louis found.

"The maintenance man, who's a bit of a car buff, swears he *heard* the Avanti which, according to him, has a distinctive sound." Uncle Barney nodded. Was I the only one who couldn't distinguish cars by their sounds? Had to be a guy thing. "If he's right, then our client lied to us."

"Wouldn't be the first time," Barney said drily.

"I hate being lied to. What if—"

"Then we'll inform the police," Barney said, anticipation my objection.

"How many Avantis do you suppose are in and around Westport?"

"Glenn's working on checking that."

"Uncle Barney, you're always a step ahead of me."

"Comes from having lived a few decades longer than you."

"What's our next move?"

"Going home and getting some sleep. I'll walk you to your car and follow you home."

"You think Sam will share with us anything they find on the coveralls?"

"Probably, since we're the one who told him about them."

"I SHOULD HAVE KNOWN better than to pin my hopes on the coveralls," I said to Glenn, who'd come to the shelter where I helped Maxi serve breakfast.

"You were supposed to wait for me at your house," Glenn said.

"I looked up and down my street. There was no one there except Maxi, who came to get me."

"Between the two of us we could have screamed loud enough to be heard all the way at the police station. So no worries," Maxi said.

I read the report Glenn brought with him from the agency. "No fingerprints on the zipper. No clothes fibers. No hair except one strand and that was synthetic."

"Synthetic?" Maxi asked.

"As from a wig," Glenn explained.

"A cheap wig. Expensive wigs are made from human hair."

"The chances of tracing this cheap wig are—"

"About as good as me winning the Hoosier lottery, which I don't even play," Glenn told Maxi.

"That's discouraging."

"There are some blood spatters on the coveralls, the same type as Ron's," I added. "But that doesn't help us in catching the killer." I sighed.

Maxi patted my arm. "You'll find other evidence. Now, who has time for some French toast?"

"I don't. I need to go home, change clothes, and report for work at Chesterton Enterprises."

"I have time," Glenn said eagerly. "Just let me walk Cybil to her car first."

SITTING AT THE COMPUTER I was beginning to think of as mine, I stared at the report I was to type. More chemistry stuff.

Kelli looked a little better this morning. She had

put on makeup and had dressed carefully. She wasn't crying and looked determined, as if she'd made some decisions. I wondered if she had a doctor's appointment. Before I could ask her the supervisor dumped an armload of files on my desk that needed to be updated and filed. How could there be so much paperwork? Paperwork that never ended? A little grumpily I set to work, hoping that we would solve this case soon and keep me from drowning under all this paper.

At lunch I met Maxi at the shelter. After discussing the pros and cons, we decided to try to locate the Maniac Messiah again. We'd tried twice before and failed. We stopped at the Church of Holiness but the Reverend Brown was out tending to the needs of his flock, as his secretary phrased it.

Maxi smiled at the grim woman. "We're actually trying to locate Calvin Laxton."

"Who?"

"Calvin Laxton, better known as Maniac Messiah," I said.

"Oh him. He's in the sanctuary dusting the pews. He does that in exchange for lunch."

Calvin turned out to be a wizened little guy who barely lifted his feet when he walked. He shuffled slowly toward us, clutching his dust rag to his chest.

Maxi decided to take the initiative. "Mr. Laxton, could you spare us a minute of your time?"

He blinked at Maxi and then nodded.

"We've been admiring the slips of scripture you hand out. Can you tell us where you get them?"

He glanced toward the secretary's office. He crooked a finger at us, motioning for us to come closer.

"I make them," he whispered.

"You do? How?"

"The reverend gave me permission to use the typewriter in my office."

"Your office?" Maxi asked, trying to mask the doubt in her voice.

"That's what I call it." He motioned for us to follow him. He shuffled down the hall, past the Sunday school classrooms, and opened a door.

Maxi and I exchanged a look after gazing into the walk-in closet which was used as a storage area. It did, however, contain a small desk and a chair. On the desk stood a black, manual typewriter that surely would feel at home in a museum.

"You still get ribbons for this typewriter?" Maxi asked. "I used to own one just like it. Purely loved it."

"I got a whole box of ribbons. They'll last me a lifetime. You see, I type the quotations only once and then I make copies on the copy machine. The reverend said I could."

"And then you hand them out to people?" Maxi asked.

"Only to some." He opened the desk drawer, picked out a strip of paper, and handed it to Maxi.

"Thank you, Mr. Laxton," she said gravely.

He nodded. "Now I have to get back to work. I got ten pews to do before lunch."

We thanked him and left.

"What does your quotation say?" I asked Maxi.

"*Blessed are those who dwell in thy house, ever singing thy praise.* It's from Psalms but I don't recall from which one."

I wasn't sure whether I should be insulted or relieved that he hadn't given me a quotation.

BACK AT WORK I NOTICED that Kelli wasn't at her desk. I checked the ladies' room but she wasn't there either.

"Debbie, have you seen Kelli?"

"Not since lunch. I came back to my desk because I'd forgotten the magazine I was going to read, when I saw her come out of Mrs. Dowd's office. She looked upset but I didn't think anything of it because the boss lady can be mean and sarcastic when you make a mistake."

"Did you speak to Kelli?"

"I was going to but she grabbed her purse and ran out of here. You don't suppose she got fired?"

I stared at Debbie, praying she was wrong. Kelli needed this job and the medical insurance that came with it. "Surely not. Kelli struck me as a very capable secretary."

"She is. Still, that hasn't kept Mrs. Dowd from firing people who did something wrong. And she's been in a bad mood, what with her husband getting killed. I was surprised she came to the office today."

I was too. And I had a bad feeling about Kelli. Getting pregnant by the boss's husband surely qualified as having done something wrong.

ELEVEN

I HAD JUST RETURNED from my coffee break next morning when Sam and Sergeant Griffin arrived in the Chesterton offices. Both nodded to me but walked straight to Margot Chesterton Dowd's office. Her secretary announced them and then shut the door behind them.

Debbie and I exchanged a look but she merely shrugged, as surprised and curious as I was. My gaze focused on Kelli's desk which looked as tidy as she'd left it the day before. Uneasily I wondered if she was sick or if she had indeed been fired.

"Did Kelli call in sick?" I asked Debbie.

"I don't know. The supervisor didn't say."

A few minutes later we watched Margot lead the two detectives to the conference room and then return to her office. Sam started to call us in one by one and I knew something was terribly wrong.

When it was my turn I sat on the edge of the chair, barely able to contain my curiosity. "Did something happen to Kelli?"

"What makes you think something happened to her?" Sam asked, his tone suspicious.

"Because you're here and she is not."

"She was killed last night by a hit-and-run driver."

"What? How awful! Poor Kelli and that baby. Oh, no." I swayed and almost fell off the chair.

Sergeant Griffin, who was closer than Sam, jumped up and laid a steadying hand on my shoulder.

"What baby?" Sam asked.

"Kelli was three months pregnant."

"How do you know that?"

"I recognized the symptoms of morning sickness and when I spoke to her she admitted being pregnant."

"Did she tell you who the father was?"

"No, but I…"

"You have a pretty good idea who he is. Out with it, Cybil."

"Ron Dowd. Why don't you run a DNA test? That'll tell you for sure."

Sam wrote something in his notebook. "That's all for now. Thanks, Cybil."

"Not so fast. I gave you vital information, so how about returning the favor. Where and when was Kelli killed?"

"Last night around nine near the shelter."

I stared at Sam. "What shelter?"

"Mercy Shelter. Your shelter."

"What?"

"You heard me."

"What was she doing in that neighborhood?"

"I have no idea. Maybe she was coming to see you."

"On a cold winter night?"

"Can you think of a better reason for her to be there?"

"No. Where was her car?"

"In the library parking lot."

"The library was closed by then so she couldn't have been there."

"Maybe she was waiting to meet someone. Or maybe she left it there because she didn't want anyone to see her at the shelter."

"Did you check her car?"

"Yup. It started without trouble. She wasn't out of gas, and she had no flat tires."

"Was she hit in the parking lot?"

"No. She was on the sidewalk just north of the library."

"That put her on the way to the shelter. Did anyone see it happen?"

"Not see it up close but heard it real good. There's a tavern a couple of blocks north of the library. A patron leaving it heard a car accelerate, saw its headlights swerve up onto the sidewalk, and then saw it speed away."

"The car made no attempt to stop?" I asked, my voice disbelieving.

"No," Sam said, his expression grim. "At first

light this morning we had an expert look at the scene. His verdict: Somebody deliberately ran her down."

I gripped the edges of my chair, for suddenly I felt dizzy and sick. "He or she killed two human beings in cold blood. Kelli and her baby," I whispered.

"Cybil, you're not going to faint on me?" Sam asked.

"No, but this is so awful…"

"We'll get the perp. That truck or SUV has to have trace evidence on it."

"A truck or SUV?"

"Could have been a small pickup. Anyway, it was an elderly black or navy vehicle in need of a tune-up, according to our witness. Unfortunately, he'd had a few beers which is something a good defense attorney is going to pounce on. We'll need other corroborating evidence."

"Kelli was a nice girl whose major mistake was to fall for a married man and get pregnant. Nobody should be run down by a car like that."

"I agree," Sam said. "And I promise we'll get the perp. Can you go back to work, or shall I call Luke to come and get you?"

"I'm okay," I said quickly, not wanting Luke to get involved. I went straight to the ladies' room where I splashed cold water on my face.

When I looked at myself in the mirror my eyes widened. Bruises had blossomed on the skin of my throat where I'd been choked by the intruder at the shelter. Quickly I buttoned the top button of my blouse but that didn't help. For the next few days I'd have to wear turtlenecks.

Several things were bothering me. I braced my hands against the wash basin and tried to line up my arguments in my mind. No matter how I arranged them they all pointed me back to the club. I had to get back there and do some talking to people, or put less elegantly, do some snooping.

I returned to my desk, grabbed my purse, and told Debbie I was taking an early lunch hour. She looked at me wide-eyed but merely nodded. In the parking lot I used my cell to phone Louis.

He was scheduled to take a lunch break in thirty minutes and would meet me at the back entrance. I offered to buy him lunch but he'd brought his from home. However, he had a special fondness for chocolate milkshakes. I knew that the Dairy Queen near the club had space for a counter and tables and thus stayed open all year. I swung through the drive-thru and bought two shakes.

As promised, Louis had parked his truck on the other side of the back entrance gate, which he unlocked for me. I joined him in his truck. We sipped our shakes for a while before I broached the subject that had brought me to the club.

"Louis, how could someone get into the club through this back entrance which is locked all the time? And please understand that I'm not accusing you of anything."

He nodded.

"Who has the keys to the gate?"

"I have one and the manager has another. We used to have a spare in the tack room but it went missing some weeks ago."

"That's interesting. How many weeks ago?"

Louis thought for a moment. "Two, I think. I reported it to the manager and suggested that we change the locks on the gate. He said he'd see to it but so far he hasn't gotten around to it."

"Who has access to the tack room?"

"Technically every member who rides here, but they have to get the riding master to unlock the room. At least it's *supposed* to be locked."

"You've found the room unlocked?"

"Yeah, several times."

"Who's the riding master?"

"Reggie Clark. Young guy. Related to the manager of the club."

Louis and I exchanged a knowing look. Nepotism. No wonder Reggie hadn't been fired for leaving the tack room unlocked.

"So just about anybody in the club could have taken the key and unlocked the back gate," I said.

"Yeah, at least those who knew where we kept the spare key. Mostly employees, I figure. Members come here to ride and enjoy themselves, not to worry with keys."

"Has a member ever tried to bribe you?"

Louis looked uneasy and squirmed in the seat. "Bribe is too strong a word. They give us tips for doing extra things for them. And it's not against the rules to accept a tip."

I nodded that I understood. Hadn't my bringing him a milkshake been a bribe of sorts? Not so very different from slipping an employee a couple of bills for unlocking the back gate, for allowing someone to park in the club's garage.

"Louis, picture the guy who posed as a maintenance man. Is there anything else you remember about him?"

He stared through the windshield, thinking. Then he shook his head. "No. He was just a guy. Short and skinny. Oh, and he had a mustache. Not much of one," Louis said, stroking his own luxurious growth above his upper lip. "That's all I remember."

"It's okay. I better let you get back to work." I left him and went searching for the riding master. Unfortunately, Reggie Clark was getting ready to give a riding lesson. The well-groomed, middle-aged woman was impatient to get started and resented me for taking up her instructor's time and attention. It used to be the tennis pro who had the ladies chasing after him, but Reggie, with his blinding, toothy smile and shock of wheat-hued hair could give him a run for his money.

Our conversation was brief and unsatisfactory. He knew nothing about the missing key. Members were going into the tack room all the time. Anyone could have taken it. I watched him swing himself into the saddle with lithe grace and youthful ease, smile at his student, and ride off.

Another dead end. Discouraged, I sat in my car for a while trying to decide what to do next.

I needed to interview Kelli's neighbors. I located her address on the city map and drove to her building.

She had lived in a large house that had been converted into apartments. Hers had been an efficiency unit on the top floor. The owner of the building, an elderly woman named Florence, invited me into her apartment. She owned two small white dogs who had a good time sniffing my pant legs. Apparently they detected the scent of Buddy, who always rubbed herself against my legs.

"Kelli was a good tenant. Always paid her rent on the first day of the month. I never had to remind her like I do some tenants. And she didn't have loud parties. Pretty much kept to herself."

"Did she have a steady boyfriend?"

"For the last four or five months the same guy came around. Older than her and probably married. Had that married look about him."

I wanted to ask her what that married look was but she didn't give me a chance. Besides, I think I knew the look she meant.

"I hinted to Kelli that there was no future in wasting time on a married man and that a girl as young and as pretty as her should concentrate on single guys, but she didn't take my hint." Florence sighed. "Can't tell the young ones anything."

I described the fake maintenance man to her. My mouth dropped open when she said he'd been around, looking for Kelli. "When was that?"

"Let me see. Must have been last week some time. I remember because I had just got back from the vet's. Bittsy had a cold."

She pointed to one of the dogs. I had no idea which one Bittsy was. They looked identical to me.

"I told him that Kelli wasn't home and probably wouldn't be until late. She had a date."

"What did the guy say?"

"Nothing. Just looked at me real mean. I was glad when he left. He gave me the creeps."

"And why was that?"

"I don't know. He had a phony kind of voice. You know, trying to sound like someone he wasn't. And there was just something mean about him. He had the kind of mustache that villains in old movies had. Kinda fake looking. I meant to warn Kelli about him but I didn't see her that evening and then I forgot. Kelli was a nice girl. I can't believe she's gone." Florence dabbed at her eyes with an embroidered hanky, the kind Maxi carried in her purse.

I couldn't bring myself to tell her that Kelli had been murdered. "Have the police been here?"

"They searched her stuff. Don't know what they were looking for. Told me her folks would come for her things some time this week and then I could rent the place again."

"Would you let me look at her apartment?"

Florence studied me for a minute. "Okay. I guess you won't run off with her things. You'll have to go up by yourself. The stairs kill my knees."

I took the key she handed me and went upstairs. Before I unlocked the door I slipped my hands into gloves.

The place was little more than one large room with a tiny kitchen and a bathroom added along the left wall. On the far end of the room a sliding-glass door led to a small balcony. I saw snow-covered wooden boxes in which Kelli must have planted flowers last spring. This small attempt at beautifying her space made me like her. Now she would never have another chance to plant flowers again. I felt like crying.

I pulled myself together and searched the room, which didn't take long. I found a prescription for prenatal vitamins which Kelli hadn't had a chance to get filled. In a rubber-banded bundle of papers marked paid bills I found a note card, the kind that the county's humane society sold as a fund-raiser. There were only six words printed on the inside:

Leave him alone, bitch, or else.

There was an envelope, postmarked Westport.

I dialed Sam's number. He picked up right away.

"Sam, did you guys see the card in Kelli's apartment, the one that warned and threatened her?"

"What card?"

I described it and where I found it.

"Did you leave your prints all over it?"

"I know better than that. I'm wearing gloves."

"Where did you find this card?"

"It was stuck in the envelope with the paid electric bill."

"What made you look there?"

"The envelope seemed too thick to contain just a bill."

"Miss Smarty Pants. And what are you doing, snooping in that apartment?"

"Florence gave me permission."

"Florence?"

"The landlady. She said you were here already and had finished. You're just mad because your men overlooked something, and I didn't. You want me to bring the note to you or leave it?"

"Leave it. I want to take another look at that apartment."

Sam, in his usual brusquely efficient manner, hung up without another word.

AT THE SHELTER THAT evening I told Glenn about the card.

"You're sure the words were typed? Not that many people have typewriters anymore."

"That's where you're wrong. Lots of people kept their typewriters. I did. They come in handy when addressing envelopes or typing something on index cards. Even the Maniac Messiah uses one. And speaking of him, have you seen him recently?"

"No. He's not a regular, but he occasionally comes for dinner."

"I haven't seen him either. Let's check with Maxi." But Maxi hadn't seen him either. Not for at least two days. "He sometimes forgets to eat," she said, her expression worried. "I'll make a sandwich and go to the church and look for him."

"I'll go with you."

Maxi fixed him a pimento cheese sandwich which she said was his favorite and filled a small thermos with sweetened tea. We bundled up and walked to the Church of Holiness. The choir was practicing and sounded good. We looked around for Maniac. Finally we knocked on the door of the supply closet he called his office.

There was no answer but I thought I heard something. I placed my finger across my lips. In silence we listened, hardly daring to breathe. Finally we heard the noise again. It was a cross between a whimper and a sob.

Maxi opened the door and turned on the light. Cowering in the corner next to the boxes of paper towels was Maniac. He placed his arms over his head in a protective gesture.

"Mr. Laxton, it's me, Maxi Keller. We met the other day. You gave me one of your quotations. And I have a quote for you. Want to hear it?"

He nodded but didn't turn around.

"'Let not your heart be troubled, neither let it be afraid.' It's from John Fourteen, remember?"

He nodded again and turned to face us. Both Maxi and I gasped. We bent down for a closer look.

"What happened to your face?" Maxi asked.

His hand covered the side of his face as if to hide the black and blue marks. He shrugged.

"Someone hit you and hit you hard," I said. "Who was it?" He turned away. "You may as well tell me now because I'll find out."

"Believe me, she will," Maxi said. "My granddaughter is a determined woman."

"The giant hit me."

"The giant?" Maxi asked.

"He hangs out around the shelter."

"Does he sometimes wear a ski mask?" I asked.

"Yeah. That's one mean dude."

"Yes, he is. Why did he hit you?"

"To keep me quiet."

"Quiet about what?"

He shook his head and looked away, his expression frightened.

"We won't tell the giant or anyone else," Maxi assured him. "I promise. What are you supposed to keep quiet about?"

"That I saw him in the shelter."

Maxi and I exchanged a puzzled look.

"Where in the shelter did you see him?" I asked.

"In the room where the men sleep."

"In the dormitory? Did he sleep there?"

"No. This was during the day when nobody is supposed to be there. I came in to mop the floor. Miss Abby told me to."

He seemed agitated. Quietly I said, "You're right. The giant wasn't supposed to be there. Did he say why he was there?"

"He just hit me and said to keep my mouth shut. He's not nice."

"No, he isn't," Maxi said gently.

Maniac touched his forehead, thinking hard. "Wait. The footlocker."

"What about the footlocker?" Maxi asked.

"He was trying to open it."

"In the dormitory? A footlocker used by one of the men?" I asked. His expression grew more agitated.

"I don't know nothin'."

"It's okay," Maxi said. "I brought you a sandwich and some tea."

"No cookie?"

"Next time I'll bring a cookie," she promised.

That seemed to soothe his agitation. We left him munching his cheese sandwich.

On our way back to the shelter, Maxi asked, "This giant. You know whom he meant?"

"Yes. I don't know his name but he's the one who's been trying to get into the shelter. Now we know why. He seems to think one of the men has something he wants or needs. We know he's succeeded in getting into the dormitory. I wonder if he got what he was looking for."

"If there are no more attempts to get in we'll know he succeeded. Otherwise he'll try again."

"What could any of the men have that's so valuable to cause repeated attempts at getting it?"

Maxi shook her head. "Most of them have little more than the clothes on their backs and what's in their pockets."

"Obviously the giant seems to think otherwise."

"One thing's for sure. From now on we need more than one person here at all times. Even with the bars over the windows, courtesy of Luke, we're not completely safe."

"That reminds me. I need to do something nice for Luke. I didn't really think he'd do it. When he said he'd get bars for the windows I thought…"

"That this was something he just said on the spur of the moment."

I nodded.

"Cybil, you of all people should know that Luke means what he says," Maxi chided softly.

Ashamed, I nodded. "I know that."

We said good-bye. Maxi insisted that I drive off first. I did, knowing she would wait me out. Since I drove north I knew she couldn't see me after the street curved. I turned around and pulled to the side of the road until I saw her leave the parking lot safely.

WHILE WORKING IN THE Chesterton office and feeling bored to tears, I spent a lot of time thinking about what I should do for Luke in exchange for the window bars. It needed to be something personal but not so personal as to make him think I wanted us to live together again.

That also brought up the problem of Christmas presents. He would probably buy me one even though I'd told him I didn't want to exchange presents. Or celebrate the holiday in any way. It was just too painful.

I looked around for the supervisor. When I didn't see her I dialed an outside number.

Sam picked up on the first ring.

"This is the second time this week that I've gotten through to you immediately. The crime business must be slow."

"I wish it were. I'm answering my phone because I'm hoping it's the lab with good news or anybody else with helpful information."

"Stuck on the Ron Dowd murder?"

"And on his girlfriend's."

"Nothing helpful on the threatening card? Fingerprints?" I asked, hoping he hadn't found Margot's prints.

Sam snorted. "We should be so lucky."

"Well, at least we know it was mailed locally by a woman."

"What makes you so sure it was a woman?"

"Come on, Sam. 'Leave him alone, bitch, or else'? Sounds like a jealous woman to me."

Sam sighed. "Could be. Doesn't help much, though. From the way he was fooling around it could be any number of women he'd known who were now jealous of Kelli."

That, unfortunately, was true.

I hung up and stared at my computer screen. What I was typing consisted either of columns of figures or formulas. Chemistry had been my least favorite subject in high school, and I had managed to avoid the subject in college only to have it catch up with me now. Blast.

Since Kelli's death, much of her work had been dumped on my desk. She had been Ron's secretary. It felt strange to type the notes he had scribbled on sheets from a yellow pad. Most of the notes dealt with chemical fertilizers. Didn't Frederick Holmes produce fertilizers? Is that what brought them together the evening I followed Ron to Classic Greens? Maybe Ron had not been blackmailing Frederick. Maybe he was selling something to the fertilizer producer? But what?

I looked intently at the formulas and columns but they meant nothing to me. Sighing in frustration, I focused on the giant and our problems at the shelter. What I needed was a photo of the man to pass around. Surely someone must know who that huge young man was. And I wasn't forgetting that he had choked me. My neck still felt tender.

On my way to the shelter after work I stopped at the nearest drugstore and bought two disposable cameras. If and when he showed up again I was going to be ready for him.

TWELVE

"SO, WHAT DO WE KNOW for sure?" Maxi asked while we waited for our breakfasts at our favorite new diner, The Hungry Cat.

"Very little," I said despondently. This morning not even the whimsical cat drawings which adorned the walls could cheer me up.

"We have two groups of dead people," Maxi continued in a matter-of-fact manner. "Duchess and friends from the shelter and two people from Chesterton Enterprises. And the assaults on you and Maniac."

"Are you suggesting that the cases are connected?" I thought for a moment. "I don't see how. The shelter and Chesterton Enterprises may as well exist on different planets."

"True," Maxi said, her expression thoughtful. She added sugar to her coffee. "We have death by poison, knife, and automobile." She took a sip of coffee and added another packet of sugar. "Duchess's killer has to be a different person."

I nodded. The waitress brought out poached eggs on whole wheat toast and refilled our cups. I stared at my food, unable to eat.

"Is something wrong with your food?"

"Everything's wrong. It's my fault Kelli is dead."

Maxi put her fork down and looked at me. "And how is the hit and run your fault?"

"I told Kelli I could help her. She was obviously on her way to see me at the shelter. If I hadn't offered help—"

"You think she'd be alive. *Unsinn.*"

"It may be nonsense but I can't help wondering."

"I'm not exactly a fatalist but some things we cannot prevent or change. Death is one of them. Remember that short story where a man learns that death waits for him at the end of his journey to a certain city so he decides to go to a different town? Of course, death is there, waiting for him."

I did remember the short story. It had the word *appointment* in the title, I seemed to recall.

"Kelli's death is not your fault."

"On a rational level I know that."

"Tell you what we'll do. We have to catch whoever killed her. Then you'll feel better. Me too. Every time I think of that baby who never had a chance I get so upset, I'd like to hit something."

"I hear you."

"So, let's review the facts and go from there."

She made a gesture, inviting me to summarize. I did.

"According to Sam's witness, a black or navy small truck or pickup or SUV deliberately ran up on the sidewalk, hit Kelli, and drove away. Sam's expert took measurements of the tire marks and agreed with the witness that this was a deliberate act."

Maxi took over. "And Kelli's lover and the father of her unborn baby was stabbed to death at the club shortly before she was hit by a car or truck."

"I think the same person killed Ron and Kelli but someone else poisoned Duchess and Mick. I mean, what are the chances that Duchess knew any of the people the Dowds know?"

"Slim to none. The problem in both cases is motive. If we even had an inkling of why harmless homeless people like Duchess and Mick were killed we might have a chance of finding their murderer."

"All I can come up with is that they saw or heard something they weren't supposed to," I said.

"Among the homeless? What dangerous bits of information or secrets could they have?"

I shrugged wearily.

"As to your client, she has a strong motive: a betrayed wife with a philandering husband. Worse—a husband who got another woman pregnant. You told me that she hired the agency to check on her husband so she suspected something but wanted to be sure. Documented infidelity would undoubtedly lower the financial settlement he'd receive in a divorce."

"But why hire us if she planned to kill him? With us in the picture she'd have to be extra careful not to make any mistakes. And if she was willing to divorce him, why take the risk of a murder charge?"

"That's a good point." Maxi ate one of her eggs before she spoke again. "Do the Dowds have children?"

"No. Debbie at the office mentioned something about Margot not being able to have kids."

"Ah."

I raised an eyebrow. "That was a very expressive 'ah.'"

"The mistress was able to give him a child when the wife was not. That must have rankled powerfully, and Margot strikes me as a proud woman."

I must have looked unconvinced, for my grandmother leaned across the table toward me.

"Remember the story in Genesis of Sarah and Hagar? How the slave woman lorded it over the wife because she bore the husband a son? Can you imagine how vindictive and mean Sarah must have been to Hagar when she finally had a son herself?"

"I never liked Sarah, and I always felt sorry for Hagar."

"Me too."

"We're assuming that Margot knew that Kelli was pregnant," I pointed out.

"Yes, and that's a big assumption. How would she have found out? From Ron? Why would he confess that? Surely he'd know that this might well end the marriage, or if he didn't care that the marriage was

over he'd have to realize that fathering an illegiti-
mate child would seriously compromise his divorce
settlement."

"If he even knew that Kelli was pregnant." Then
I remembered something Kelli had said.

"What?"

"When I asked Kelli about her finances she said
something like she knew how to get money. And this
was after Ron's death."

"Ah. If she went to Margot and demanded money
she would have had to tell her about Ron's baby."
Maxi toyed with a triangle of toast. "But why would
Margot give Kelli money? She wasn't legally obli-
gated to do so."

"What if Kelli threatened to boast who the father
of her baby was? As you said, Margot is a proud
woman."

"And she certainly wouldn't miss a reasonable
amount of money."

"Yes, but then why kill Kelli if she could buy her
off?"

Maxi shook her head. "I don't know. Maybe Margot couldn't control her anger over the betrayal. We
need to remember what powerful emotions betrayal
can bring up."

We were both silent. Finally Maxi spoke.

"I'm sorry. I'm not helping your case, only making it worse."

"Not your fault that it looks bad for Margot."

"You have anyone else who might have had a reason to eliminate Ron?"

"There are probably husbands and boyfriends out there who're not shedding any tears over his death. And Ron and Frederick Holmes had a bitter argument. Frederick handed Ron a bunch of money. Could be a legitimate payment. A consultant's fee. Ron was a chemist. Or it could be payment for…" I shrugged. "I thought of telling Sam but I have no proof that anything criminal went down."

"Tell him anyway."

My grandmother was right. I'd call Sam on my coffee break. Suddenly I was hungry. The eggs looked good.

AFTER WORK I FORCED myself to go to the mall to do some Christmas shopping. As expected I didn't do so well. Both Maxi and Luke are hard to buy for. For my mother I found some fancy bath salts and a book on the Maldive Islands. She and my stepfather were planning a trip over the holidays to somewhere warm and exotic and what's more exotic than a bunch of islands near India and Sri Lanka? I was ready to bet that no one in her circle of acquaintances was going there or had ever been.

I dashed home—well, not dashed exactly as it was snowing again—and accessed the islands on the Internet. They were perfect. Come February when we were all weary of the phenomenon known as lake effect snow that regularly dumped tons of the white stuff on northern Indiana, I wouldn't mind a trip to these islands myself. Unfortunately, my budget didn't include a travel fund.

I printed the information and drove to my mother's house. She opened the door herself. I wondered if she was between maids again.

"Well, hello, Cybil. I didn't expect to see you again so soon."

"You look great, Mom." And she did. She wore black silk slacks which couldn't have been larger than a size four and a shimmery turquoise blouse that accented her blond beauty.

"Thank you."

I followed her into the living room. "Justin not home yet?"

"He's meeting a client. Actually, someone you know, Frederick Holmes. Didn't you meet him here?"

"Yes. Mom, I found the perfect spot for you and Justin to go for your Christmas vacation. The Maldives."

She raised a perfectly arched brow. "Where on earth is that?"

"A group of islands in the Indian Ocean near India and Sri Lanka with incredible blue water and miles of white, sandy beaches. It's apparently great for snorkeling which is something you and Justin love to do."

"Isn't it awfully out of the way and probably primitive?"

"It has eighty-six tourist resorts. The Maldives have become a hot vacation spot for Europeans."

"What language do they speak?"

"Lots of people speak English since the islands were a British protectorate until 1965. I bet no one in your social circle has been there."

"Probably not."

"Here. I brought you a book on the island and a printout. It was composed by a travel agency so it tells a prospective visitor everything he or she needs to know."

"Thank you, Cybil." She looked a little down.

"What's wrong, Mom?"

She shrugged. "I don't know how much attention you pay to the economy but it's a little depressed right now. That's what Justin is meeting with Frederick about."

"Classic Greens isn't doing well?"

"Nobody is doing as well as they'd like."

Especially if they had to pay hefty sums to a blackmailer. "I'm sorry. I'm so used to dealing with clients at the shelter who haven't done well, to put it mildly, in a long time so that I don't pay much attention to the economy. Although eventually the effects of economic trends filter down to the shelter."

"I'll keep the information. Maybe next year. But why don't you go?"

"Mom, I'm a salaried employee. By the time I make my mortgage payment and pay my bills I'm lucky if I can afford to go to the Chicago Symphony a few times a year."

"You wouldn't have to be on such a tight budget if you played your cards right. Luke is a successful physician—"

"Mom!"

"Okay, okay. I'm just pointing out that you have options."

"Thanks but I'm doing fine." Time to make my escape. I left a few minutes later.

It wasn't that I didn't still have feelings for my husband. I did. I had no desire to date any other man. I just needed to be on my own for a while. I had married Luke right after my graduation from college. After he finished his residency we'd been blessed with our sweet little boy. I'd thought my life was all mapped out for me but death had had a different idea.

Don't dwell on it.

I took some deep breaths. I hadn't practiced my hatha yoga positions and relaxation in days and the tension in my body told me so. I resolved to have a good session when I got home.

First I had to go to the shelter. Pete was on duty and glad to see me. While we washed the pots and pans we talked a little.

"I haven't seen you in a while," I said.

"Miss Abby set up a workshop in the empty house for making things to sell."

"Oh yeah? Things like what?"

"Well, my contribution is a bird feeder that you either hang from a tree or balcony or mount on a pole."

I stared at him for a moment. "How absolutely perfect. I hope you have two left? One for my grandmother and one for Luke. He has a balcony. I think the ones on a stand would be perfect for Maxi."

"We still have a bunch of them. They're on sale at the church."

"I'm going right over there before they're all gone."

"Mrs. Quindt, I promised Glenn not to let you out of my sight."

"Where is he?"

"He hurried off, saying something about a big guy."

"Maniac's giant." I hoped Glenn wasn't going to confront the huge man by himself.

"If you want me to I'll go to the church with you," Pete offered shyly.

"That would be great." I drove us to the church and bought three bird feeders. May as well put one outside my sliding-glass door to give Buddy something to watch.

We loaded the feeders into my trunk and headed back to the shelter.

"Where did you learn your woodworking skills?

Were you a carpenter in—" I stopped, horrified. I had broken the unwritten rule of not prying into our clients' lives. "I'm sorry."

"It's okay. I had an uncle who built furniture after work to relax. I used to go to his house. When he saw that I was interested he taught me stuff." Pete paused for a moment. "In my life before I ended up on the street, I was a chemist."

We had just gotten back to the shelter when Glenn burst into the kitchen, breathing hard.

"What happened?" I asked.

"I almost caught up with Maniac's giant but the young man is quick and nimble. Despite his size he can move."

"So he's still coming around."

"Yup. That's one persistent cuss. I'm going to check the neighborhood again. He's around here somewhere. Failing that, maybe I'll discover his shortcuts."

"Be careful." I knew Glenn was carrying a handgun but I also knew he'd use it only most reluctantly.

Pete hovered near me in the kitchen as if he wanted to speak to me. I waited and started to peel the potatoes I'd boiled earlier for tomorrow's hash browns.

"Mrs. Quindt, if I give you money, will you mail something for me?"

"Sure." The main post office was only a couple of blocks from the shelter. I stopped myself from asking why he didn't do it himself. Abby had told me when I first started at the shelter that our clients were reluctant to have anything to do with authority figures and official buildings.

Pete pulled a thick envelope from under his coat and handed it to me along with five crumpled single dollar bills.

"How do you want me to mail this?"

"I don't know," he said, a little embarrassed. "Is there a way which will prove that it was mailed?"

"The simplest way is to send it delivery confirmation. You'll get a form with an eight hundred number on it which you can call in a few days and it'll tell you exactly when the enveloped was delivered."

"Okay, can you mail it delivery confirmation?"

"Sure."

"Is that enough money?"

"I should get some change back."

"Thank you. I appreciate that. Good night."

He waited outside until I got into my car and drove off.

I couldn't help but glance at the address on the envelope. I almost drove up on the sidewalk when I saw that Pete was sending something to the patent office in Washington, DC.

FIRST THING I DID THE next day was mail Pete's envelope. I placed the green-and-white receipt with the eight hundred number and the change into an envelope to give to Pete. I hoped that whatever it was he sent to the patent office would turn his life around.

From the post office I went to the police station. I caught Sam on his way out.

"You know the big guy who broke into the shelter and choked me?"

"Yeah?"

"He keeps disappearing into the buildings near the shelter which leads me to believe he knows the area really well. What are my chances of getting a map of the neighborhood?"

Sam wagged his hand, suggesting my chances were so-so. "Those five or six blocks are full of abandoned buildings. Or buildings that are in use as storage facilities. I'm not even sure that the map the city planning commission has is one hundred percent accurate."

"My best chance of getting a map would be from the planning commission?"

Sam shrugged. "That's as good a place as any to start."

Since the planning commission had its offices downtown I walked there. Looking at the posted list of the members, I was surprised to see that Frederick Holmes was one of them. The man got around. I had prepared a lengthy explanation as to why I wanted to look at the records but the young woman in the office wasn't particularly interested in my reasons. She let me look at the records. Nor did she object when I drew simple versions of the floor plans in my notebook. I thanked her and drove to the shelter.

Glenn was there. Over cups of coffee we looked at my sketches.

"Interesting that originally the two corner buildings were one building," I said.

"They were a factory where they built horse-drawn buggies and farm wagons. Later they switched to building automobiles," Glenn told me.

"Really?"

"Yeah. Real classic beauties. Some were custom-designed for movie stars and society people."

"Since the buildings were connected, our giant obviously found a door leading from one building to the other. I wonder where he got a key to get in?"

"Maybe picking locks is one of his specialties."

"If that were so, he wouldn't have had to kick in the kitchen door," I said, pointing to our new door.

"I'd forgotten he did that. I wish we knew what he was after."

"Or whom. It could be a person."

Glenn nearly dropped his coffee cup. "It just occurred to me that maybe he's responsible for the deaths at the shelter."

I felt the blood rush to my head. "Duchess? You think he might have poisoned her? Would she have accepted food from a stranger?"

"If he'd plied her with alcohol first. Remember, the autopsy report showed that she'd been drinking."

"But what possible reason could he have for killing these poor, homeless people?"

"That's the sixty-four-dollar question. Unless he just dislikes them."

"That's insane!"

"Exactly."

"Now you're creeping me out," I said and shuddered.

"I hope so." He looked at me sternly. "Cybil, remember you can't come to the shelter by yourself. Your grandmother either. The guy's ruthless." Glenn paused. Then lifting his index finger for emphasis, he said, "I'm going to take you to the shooting range and turn you into a first-class marksman. Markswoman."

I don't like the sound of that; I don't like guns. If it were up to me I'd make it extremely difficult for people to buy guns. "Uncle Barney isn't going to allow me to carry a gun yet."

"He will once you have your PI license. It takes lots of practice to become a crack shot. May as well start."

I made one of those noncommittal sounds that could mean either agreement or disagreement.

AT NOON I MET MAXI at the shelter to give her a ride to the Holmes house. Brittany had invited us and seven other women to lunch. She was hosting a series of these fund-raising meals. We were served box lunches.

I looked at the miniature croissant filled with mayonnaise-laden chicken salad and whispered to Maxi, "For what we paid for this food they could at least have given us regular-sized croissants and chicken salad that wasn't mainly mayo."

Maxi patted my hand. "It's for a good cause. You know how long we've waited for the youth activity center. This will bring it one step closer."

"You're right. If I hadn't skipped breakfast I wouldn't have noticed the size of the croissant. My fault."

"What was so urgent that you had to skip breakfast?"

I told my grandmother about my morning.

"I remember when those buildings housed the car factories. This was before Michigan cornered the automobile manufacturing market. In those days there were several small companies that built custom-designed cars. When they closed, the town almost died economically." Maxi sighed, remembering those hard times.

"Glenn told me about that. Westport must have been a hopping place back then."

"Yes, but it also had its down side. There was a tavern on every corner of Main Street and they were busy every night, not just on Saturday. The air quality wasn't the best and traffic at the end of each shift was horrendous. But the men had jobs so I guess it was a tradeoff."

I sensed before I saw movement at the door. By the time I looked up the figure had passed but I knew that silhouette. "Excuse me," I said. "The ladies' room." I hurried into the hall, just in time to see the last door on the right close. Without hesitation I ran to it and opened it. Only afterwards did it occur to me that this might have been a bathroom. Fortunately, it was the pantry. The hulking figure stood there, opening a bag of chocolate chip cookies. He looked guilty and started to put it back.

"Don't let me stop you," I said with a smile. "I was just looking for the bathroom."

"Across the hall," he said, gesturing.

I studied him, mentally measuring his size. There was no doubt in my mind that this was Maniac's giant and my assailant. I didn't think he recognized me. For one thing, at the shelter I usually wore my hair up or in a ponytail. Today I was wearing it in loose waves. And I was dressed up and wearing light makeup. I prayed he didn't recognize me. In any case, I had no choice but to brazen it out.

"Your stepmother told me that you like to walk."

He shrugged. "Helps me keep in shape." He stared at me with his pale-colored, slightly protuberant eyes. "As I said, the bathroom is across the hall."

I turned and went into the bathroom. I leaned

against the sink and concentrated on breathing in and out. The door opened and Maxi came in.

"Are you okay?" she asked, her bright blue eyes filled with concern.

I nodded and took two more deep breaths before I spoke. "Brittany's stepson is our intruder. Maniac's giant."

"Mercy." Maxi's hands flew to her chest in the classic gesture of alarm. "Are you sure?"

I nodded. "But I have no proof. It would be my word against his and that's not good enough."

Maxi nodded. "We'll think of something. Right now we better return to the luncheon."

We did in time to accept cups of coffee. The dark brew at least was excellent.

The coffee was followed by a presentation on the progress of the youth activity center. With any luck groundbreaking should commence next June. That was good news.

After the program, I walked out with Maxi.

"I know a shortcut back to the highway. Follow me, Schatzi."

I did. It had begun to snow again during our meal. The snowflakes were thick and heavy, making it hard for my windshield wipers to keep up. Squinting through the snow, I followed my grandmother. Since her farm wasn't far from the Holmeses' estate, I trusted she knew where she was going.

Seeing her brake lights and turn signal come on,

I followed her and came to a stop in front of an old barn. I ran to her pickup and scooted in beside her.

"Where are we?" I asked.

"I think we're still on the Holmeses' property. I missed the turnoff back there," Maxi admitted sheepishly.

"So this barn is theirs?"

"I think so."

"I'm going to take a look at it."

Maxi followed me.

"Look," I said, pointing to the ground where faint indentations revealed that a vehicle had been here since the last major snowfall. The main gate was padlocked as was the smaller side door.

I pointed to a window but it was too high up to allow me to look inside.

"Oma, can you back up your pickup to this window? I bet if I climb on it I can see inside."

"I can do that." She hurried back to her truck.

Using my hands to signal, I guided her as close to the barn as possible without hitting it. She got out to watch me.

I swung myself onto the bed of the pickup. With my gloves I wiped the snow off the window. It was pretty dark inside but after my eyes adjusted I saw a pickup inside. Its color was dark. Possibly forest green. I memorized the license plate number before I joined Maxi and told her what I'd seen.

"Could this be the truck that hit Kelli?" Maxi asked, her voice excited.

"It could be. It's dark colored and sort of dilapidated." I thought I caught movement in my peripheral vision. Casually I looked around. Although I didn't see anyone I felt uneasy, as if someone was watching us. "We better get out of here. I don't want another encounter with that big guy."

"Right. I don't like the vibes here," Maxi said. She, too, glanced around on her way to her pickup.

I followed her to the turnoff on the county road where she drove south and I north. I kept glancing into my rearview mirror but couldn't catch anyone following me. That didn't mean that no one was—only that I didn't have a lot of practice spotting a clever tail.

In town I headed for the maze of one-way streets that forms the center of Westport. I timed my driving speed so that I slid through every amber light, cutting off anyone who might be following me. On a light just changing to red, I turned onto my street.

For once I used the alley so that I could pull into my garage. I watched from its small, dusty window until my feet threatened to freeze to the ground. No one came. After a while I ran into my house, double-locking the door behind me.

THIRTEEN

MY NIGHT HAD BEEN UNEASY, filled with unsettling dreams in which I was pursued down snowy roads by a big man. It didn't take an analyst to tell me what that dream meant.

Feeling restless, I decided that a cold winter morning was a good time to do some baking. Nothing fancy. Nothing that required intense concentration. Something that kept my hands busy and my mind free to think. Or not. The results were blueberry muffins and an apricot-almond coffee cake which I intended to give to Luke.

I divided the muffins into two bags and took them to the police station. One I gave to Sergeant Griffin and one to Sam.

"This wouldn't be a bribe, would it?" Sam asked.

"Me? Bribe you? Never."

"But you do want something."

"I forgot to tell you something."

Sam raised a blond eyebrow. "So it's confession time." He polished off his first muffin and reached for another. Then he made that let's-hear-it motion with his hand. So I told him about Frederick Holmes giving Ron a bunch of money.

"How much money do you estimate changed hands?" he asked.

I knew exactly how much but was not ready to confess to our breaking into Ron's computer. "Several thousand. Maybe as much as five," I said.

"Legitimate?"

"I don't know, but if it was legitimate why not do it at the office during regular hours instead of meeting outdoors on a cold winter evening?"

"Blackmail?" Sam asked.

"Could be. Or a bribe. Or industrial espionage. Ron was a chemist and Frederick produces fertilizer which uses chemicals."

"Ron worked for the chemical division of Chesterton Enterprises. Did he own part of the company?"

"No. His wife owns a chunk of it but most belongs to Ron's father-in-law."

"So, not having a share in the company, Ron could have sold secrets?"

"He didn't mind cheating on his marriage so I don't think he'd be overly scrupulous about cheating on the company that employed him."

"He and Holmes could be partners in crime who had a falling out. Happens all the time."

"Does that mean Margot isn't your only suspect anymore?"

"A neighbor says she saw Mrs. Dowd return home at about the time your client said she did."

I smiled, relieved. "So Margot has an alibi for the time her husband was stabbed?"

"Seems that way, though the neighbor is near-sighted." Sam shrugged.

I could tell that this didn't make Sam happy. "You're back to square one."

"Yeah." For consolation he took another muffin.

"Maybe not. Can you find out if Frederick was at the club that morning?"

Sam looked at me for a long moment but then made a note on a yellow legal pad.

"There's something else I have to tell you. Remember the big guy who choked me and keeps lurking around the shelter?"

Sam nodded.

"I'm pretty sure it's Cameron Holmes. Frederick's son."

"Tell me about it."

I did. "But I have no proof. Except there is a pickup in their barn that could be the one that struck Kelli." That really got his attention.

"And why would father and son be after Ron's girlfriend?"

"I think she might have taken over Ron's collection policy. When I asked her if she needed help financially she hinted at having a money source." I didn't tell Sam that at first I'd thought Margot was that source.

"I know you need a good reason for a search warrant and my suspicions aren't strong enough to get one, but I'm pretty sure Cameron uses a back road to get his truck in and out of the barn. If the truck was used to run down Kelli, wouldn't there be minute traces on it even if he'd washed it since then?"

"You know this back road?"

"Maxi and I drove on it. Hand me a piece of paper and a pen." Sam did, and I drew him a map. Pointing to a landmark on the map, I said, "He probably accesses the county road here. There's a boarded-up service station across the highway that's perfect for a stakeout. You could park a patrol car there and no one would see it."

"Yes, but I can't tie up a unit in a stakeout for an indefinite number of hours and nights on your suspicions."

But I could do the stakeout. And though it was boring to sit in a car for hours, the end result would be worth it. Of course, I didn't tell Sam that.

"Any idea why Cameron is hanging out at the shelter?"

"Well, he works part-time as a bouncer at the Aces High Club which is down the street. But he's also looking for something at the shelter." I told Sam of my conversation with Maniac. I watched his reaction which was to study the ceiling of his office as if it had magically assumed the splendors of the Sistine Chapel. "Maniac's more lucid and rational than you give him credit for," I said, my voice defensive.

"Do you know how little sense it makes for someone to break into a homeless shelter repeatedly?"

"I know."

"Someone who's a successful businessman's son? What does Cameron know about the shelter and his clients?"

"Well, his father volunteers there and he talks to the men." Thinking out loud, I added, "And Ron was a chemist and so is Pete who's a client there and Frederick uses stuff that chemists invent. All coincidence? I think not." I watched Sam. Sulky teenagers hadn't a prayer of competing with Sam when it came to rolling their eyes.

"This time you're really reaching, Cybil."

"Maybe." I sighed. "Enjoy the rest of the muffins," I said and left.

LATE THAT AFTERNOON, just as it was getting dark, I parked next to the boarded-up service station. I had a large thermos of hot tea on the passenger seat and an avocado, black bean, and corn salad in a plastic container in case I got hungry.

By 7:30 I was ravenous and ate the salad, all the while staring through the windshield. Nothing happened. I sat there, most of the time shivering, until ten o'clock. Then I drove home, wondering if Sam was right and I was really reaching.

Still I continued my vigils. On the third night I was so tired I almost missed Cameron. Also, he was driving down the country road without his headlights on. He obviously didn't want anyone at his house to see him leave.

Using my cell phone, I called Sam and reported what was happening. He said he'd get the nearest patrol car to follow Cameron but would not stop him unless there was a legitimate reason. Sam promised to keep me informed.

Slowly I drove north toward the shelter. I kept a sharp eye out for the flashing lights of a police cruiser by the side of the road behind Cameron's truck but saw nothing. Needless to say I was disappointed.

In town I drove through the parking lot of the Aces High Club. I spotted Cameron's truck. Apparently it was his night to work. I parked next to his truck and phoned Sam.

"Your officer found no reason to stop Cameron?"

"He was called to a car accident where someone was hurt and had to quit the surveillance."

I could understand that but wasn't ready to give up. Taking my flashlight, I walked to the truck and inspected it. "Sam, I'm no expert but the right front headlight seems to be new. It's different from the left one. Wasn't Kelli hit with the passenger side of a truck? And wouldn't there be bits of evidence on this truck even if several days had passed and it had been washed? Surely the Westport PD is clever enough to come up with a reason to look at this truck?"

"Give me the license plate number again," Sam said, his voice sulky.

I walked to the back of the truck. "Well, what do you know? One of the tail lights is broken."

"Cybil, tell me you didn't just kick it out."

"No. I might have if I'd thought of it but I didn't. And it's definitely broken." I read him the license plate numbers.

"When does the club close?"

"At two, I think. And you better send two officers. This guy is at least six-foot-four, and I can't even begin to guess his weight. It wouldn't surprise me if he were a thoroughly bad-tempered person."

"You're full of cheerful information," Sam snapped.

"Just trying to help those who serve and protect." I hung up quickly, sensing that Sam's mood was plummeting into the grouchy region.

I THOUGHT ABOUT HANGING around but I was tired of sitting in cold cars. Besides, Sam would have a fit if he saw me. Also, I still had to deliver the coffee cake to Luke. I had no idea what shift he was working. Not that it mattered because he often stayed at the hospital whether he was on duty or not. Just in case, I'd check his apartment first.

His car was parked in his slot at his apartment building. Part of me was glad I would see him and part of me dreaded the encounter, for I never knew what emotions would surface when the two of us met. And always there was that dangerous undercurrent of attraction that threatened the fragile bond of civility we'd forged. I wished that we could be just friends and maybe some day we would be, but we weren't there yet.

I heard music from his apartment. A concerto by Bach? Probably. I knocked. The music was turned down and moments later Luke opened the door. Wearing jeans and a plaid flannel shirt, I thought he looked appealing enough to grace the cover of one of those outdoor magazines that dealt with hiking or fishing.

"I brought you a coffee cake," I blurted out. "For the window bars at the shelter. Not that this is compensation enough but it's a start."

"Thank you, Cybil. Come in, please."

I did, even though I knew I ought not to.

"Have you had any more trouble at the shelter?"

"No. Sam might be arresting the guy who bothered us as we speak."

"Good. Take your coat?"

"I can't stay." Then I saw the Christmas tree he'd put up. How could he? I couldn't bear the thought of celebrating Christmas without our little boy and Luke had put up a tree. "You have a Christmas tree," I said, my voice accusing.

"As far as I know that's not a crime. It's something most people in our society do at this time of the year."

"You know what I meant."

"Yes, I do, but life goes on no matter what happens to us."

"Life goes on? It's that simple for you?"

"There's nothing simple about it. I suspect you've always thought that I take Ryan's death more lightly than you but that's not true."

"I don't think that. You're just less demonstrative and emotional. A guy thing, I suspect."

"And a physician thing. We're trained to keep a tight control over our feelings. Otherwise we couldn't do our job."

I nodded. I held out the cake box. Luke took it. As he did his hand touched mine. I jerked it away as if I'd touched a live wire.

"There always was this spark between us. Remember?"

I nodded again.

"And some of it, a good deal of it, is still there," he said softly. "And if you deny that, you're lying."

"I'm not denying it. But it's too soon," I said and inched toward the door.

"Would you like a cup of tea? I have some of that jasmine tea you like."

"No, thank you. I can't stay."

"You're afraid to be alone with me, aren't you? Afraid of what might happen between us."

"No, that's not true." I tried to sound convincing.

"Cybil, you always were a poor liar, and I can tell when you're not telling the truth. Like now."

I opened the door.

"I'm a patient man. One of these days you'll get tired of running. I can wait," he called after me as I rushed down the stairs.

I didn't need nor did I want Luke to complicate my life. I kept telling myself that all the way to my car. I didn't exactly run but I sure walked fast and not only because it was cold.

When I reached my car I saw that I had two flat tires. How was that possible? Just after Thanksgiving I had my snow tires put on. They were practically new. Muttering some strong words I reached for my cell phone.

"Don't," a voice behind me said. "Put the phone back and get into that truck."

From my self-defense class I remembered the instructor's emphatic warnings not to get into a car or truck as that drastically diminishes the chances for survival.

"Get in," he repeated.

The voice sounded familiar. "You slashed my tires."

"Yes. Get into the truck. I'm not telling you again."

"I don't think so."

"What?"

"I said no."

"I can shoot you here and now."

"And bring half the neighborhood running before you can get away? This apartment complex has a good neighborhood watch. Listen."

"I don't hear anything."

"Exactly. A shot would be heard loud and clear." I was praying that he didn't have a silencer on his gun. I turned. "Mr. Holmes. I thought it was you. No disguise tonight? You had everyone fooled at the club with that fake hair and phony voice."

"You meddling bitch. Because of you my son is being questioned at the police station right now."

"Wrong. He's being questioned because he's a cold-blooded killer. What did you do to turn him into one?"

Frederick hauled off and slapped me. The force of his hand knocked me back a step. Fire exploded in my face, and I felt as if my head was halfway dislodged from my neck.

"I did nothing wrong. I raised him right," he claimed.

"Then he was born a killer?"

"He only wants to please me."

"So he kills for you?"

"No! Get in the truck."

I shook my head. "Tell me, what is hurting or killing me going to do for your son or for you? It'll only get you deeper into trouble."

"We're going to the shelter and then you're going to get something for me from the dormitory."

"From Pete's footlocker?" I knew now where this was heading.

"Yes."

"Too late. I mailed his patent application several days ago."

"You bitch!"

He stopped closer, undoubtedly to hurt me again, but coming closer was a mistake. I kicked him right in the crotch. He staggered back. I delivered another well-aimed kick. He clutched himself, moaning, and went down into the snow.

I had no trouble taking the gun from him. Then I punched in Sam's number.

When Frederick's moans grew fainter, I asked, "What's this patent for that is worth killing people over?"

"A new fertilizer that would put me out of business."

"And that was worth the life of Duchess? Why?"

"She caught Cameron searching the men's lockers and she told her friends."

"What about Ron Dowd and Kelli?"

"Blackmailers, both. Ron knew I'd stolen a formula and he told Kelli. I wasn't about to live my life putting up with blackmail."

"But it wouldn't bother you to spend your life

as a murderer? And turning your son into a killer as well?"

In the distance I heard the police sirens. Help was on the way.

WHEN IT WAS ALL OVER, when the police cars had left, I walked the short distance to the river. In the moonlight the water looked black. I gazed into its inky depth and felt a heavy sadness settle over me. Fathers and sons. Mothers and sons.

As I stood there, it started to snow again—thick, heavy flakes that in minutes covered everything with an immaculate white veil. Ryan would have loved this winter wonderland.

On my way home, I would stop at the Christmas tree lot and buy the biggest evergreen tree they had left, the kind of tree my son would have wanted.

* * * * *

REQUEST YOUR FREE BOOKS!

2 FREE NOVELS
PLUS 2 FREE GIFTS!

MYSTERY

WORLDWIDE LIBRARY®
Your Partner in Crime

YES! Please send me 2 FREE novels from the Worldwide Library® series and my 2 FREE gifts (gifts are worth about $10). After receiving them, if I don't wish to receive any more books, I can return the shipping statement marked "cancel." If I don't cancel, I will receive 4 brand-new novels every month and be billed just $5.24 per book in the U.S. or $6.24 per book in Canada. That's a saving of at least 34% off the cover price. It's quite a bargain! Shipping and handling is just 50¢ per book in the U.S. and 75¢ per book in Canada.* I understand that accepting the 2 free books and gifts places me under no obligation to buy anything. I can always return a shipment and cancel at any time. Even if I never buy another book, the two free books and gifts are mine to keep forever.

414/424 WDN FEJ3

Name _____ (PLEASE PRINT) _____

Address _____ Apt. # _____

City _____ State/Prov. _____ Zip/Postal Code _____

Signature (if under 18, a parent or guardian must sign)

Mail to the **Reader Service:**
IN U.S.A.: P.O. Box 1867, Buffalo, NY 14240-1867
IN CANADA: P.O. Box 609, Fort Erie, Ontario L2A 5X3

Not valid for current subscribers to the Worldwide Library series.

Want to try two free books from another line?
Call 1-800-873-8635 or visit www.ReaderService.com.

* Terms and prices subject to change without notice. Prices do not include applicable taxes. Sales tax applicable in N.Y. Canadian residents will be charged applicable taxes. Offer not valid in Quebec. This offer is limited to one order per household. All orders subject to credit approval. Credit or debit balances in a customer's account(s) may be offset by any other outstanding balance owed by or to the customer. Please allow 4 to 6 weeks for delivery. Offer available while quantities last.

Your Privacy—The Reader Service is committed to protecting your privacy. Our Privacy Policy is available online at www.ReaderService.com or upon request from the Reader Service.

We make a portion of our mailing list available to reputable third parties that offer products we believe may interest you. If you prefer that we not exchange your name with third parties, or if you wish to clarify or modify your communication preferences, please visit us at www.ReaderService.com/consumerchoice or write to us at Reader Service Preference Service, P.O. Box 9062, Buffalo, NY 14269. Include your complete name and address.

WWLI1B